CALL ME SUNFLOWER

Praise for *Call Me Sunflower*

"*Call Me Sunflower* is one of those rare books that settles into your very core and stays with you long after you finish the last page. Sunny's story will captivate your heart, oftentimes break it, but ultimately heal it together with a warm hug filled with the promise of hope."—Brooks Benjamin, author of *My Seventh-Grade Life in Tights*

"Sunny's story is heartfelt and hopeful, and it's a poignant reminder that families don't have to be perfect to be full of love." —Gail Nall, author of *Breaking the Ice* and *Out of Tune*

"Readers will be both heartbroken and warmed by the way Sunny views the world and her attempts to change it. This is a story of love, family, resilience, and grief—themes that resonate with many. Sunny is a relatable heroine with a noble cause that readers won't soon forget." —Erin Entrada Kelly, 2018 Newbery Award Winner and author of *Hello, Universe*

"A beautifully told and at times poignant story about how difficult it can be for children to navigate their changing world. Franklin's Sunflower is a lovable, creative character, and her attempts to reunite her parents, make new friendships, and form a bond with her grandmother will have readers glued to the page and heartened by the story's themes of love and resilience." —Wendy McLeod MacKnight, author of *It's a Mystery, Pig Face!*

CALL ME SUNFLOWER

MIRIAM SPITZER FRANKLIN

Sky Pony Press
New York

Sky Pony Press books may be purchased in bulk at special discounts for sales promotion, corporate gifts, fund-raising, or educational purposes. Special editions can also be created to specifications. For details, contact the Special Sales Department, Sky Pony Press, 307 West 36th Street, 11th Floor, New York, NY 10018 or info@skyhorsepublishing.com.

Sky Pony® is a registered trademark of Skyhorse Publishing, Inc.®, a Delaware corporation.

"To Be or Not to Be" Longterm Problem #3 printed with permission of Odyssey of the Mind®, a Creative Competitions, Inc. program

Visit our website at www.skyponypress.com
Books, authors, and more at www.skyponypressblog.com

www.miriamspitzerfranklin.com

10 9 8 7 6 5 4 3 2 1

Library of Congress Cataloging-in-Publication Data available on file.

Jacket image and design by Sammy Yuen

Paperback ISBN: 978-1-5107-3914-7
Ebook ISBN: 978-1-5107-1181-5

Printed in the United States of America

To Eliana and Carissa

May you always reach for the sun.

CHAPTER ONE

On my first day of sixth grade, one thought pounded louder and louder in my head as I walked up the front steps of Evergreen Middle School: *I need a plan—a really awesome, amazing plan.* One that would bring my parents back together and move us back home to New Jersey where we could be a family again, the way it was supposed to be.

I looked up at the old brick building looming in front of me. All three stories seemed to be staring down at me, threatening, and if you think buildings can't glare, then you've never seen this one. I could almost hear the low, rumbling voice: *Hey, little sixth grader! Go back to elementary school where you belong!*

If it were up to me, I'd do exactly that. I'd be starting sixth grade at Alexander Elementary with my best friend, Madeline, in a nice, friendly little school that would never growl at me.

Tugging on the straps of my backpack, I forced myself to move my feet forward.

And that's another reason I couldn't just continue moaning and groaning. I had to come up with a solution—a fail-proof plan to get Mom and Scott back together—and then I could wave goodbye and good riddance to Bennetsville, North Carolina, forever.

Mom and I stopped at the office to get my schedule. I stared out the large glass window at the swarm of kids zooming this way and that.

"Do you want me to walk with you, Sunny?" Mom asked.

Yes, yes, yes! I screamed inside my head, but I didn't notice any other parents walking their children to class so I said as maturely as I could, "I guess I can find the room myself."

"Are you sure?" Mom had that concerned look on her face, the one that came with droopy eyebrows and a turned-down mouth. Not that I was falling for it. She hadn't seemed too worried about me at the beginning of the summer when she announced we were leaving Scott and moving in with Grandma Grace, someone I only saw once a year. And all just so Mom could work on some fancy new degree.

I nodded at my mom and hiked my backpack over my shoulder. She gave me a hug, but I squirmed out of it quickly. "Mrs. Honeycutt said it's right around the corner," Mom reminded me. "The first hall you come to—"

"I'll figure it out." I took a deep breath and gave her a little wave, then turned and threw myself into the crowded maze of hallways.

I wasn't feeling brave at all, but I figured no one needed to know that. I squared my shoulders and lifted my head up, scanning the doorways for Room 117. Unfortunately, it wasn't right around the corner like the secretary had said. By the time I found the correct room number, the bell had already rung and I had to make my unplanned grand entrance.

"First day tardies are excused, but after today I expect you to be on time," said Miss Clements, my homeroom and English teacher. She glanced at my schedule, then pulled out a pencil, which had been tucked behind her ear, and made a mark on the roll. "Okay, I have you right here. Sunflower Beringer."

Whispers and muffled giggles filled the room. Someone coughed. My cheeks blazed and the tips of my ears burned. "Sunny," I managed to say. The only person who could still get away with calling me Sunflower was Scott. "I go by Sunny."

"Okay, Sunny it is," Miss Clements said, directing me to an empty seat in the front row before moving on to homeroom business. There were a few more snorts, which she ignored but I couldn't. When no one knows anything about you, a weird name doesn't help one bit.

Mom had named me Sunflower when she adopted me as a single parent, and when I was little I didn't mind it at all. It felt kind of special that I was named after a flower. All the girls in preschool were jealous and started calling themselves names like Lily and Daisy and even Chrysanthemum, after a mouse in a story we all loved. But by the time we started kindergarten, everyone had outgrown their flower names, even me. That's when I started asking people to call me Sunny, and everyone had stuck to it except Scott.

After Miss Clements answered all the first-day questions, she clapped her hands together. "Enough. Sixth graders, you'll figure it out before long. I'll assign lockers at the end of class. Let's get started with an activity to help us get to know one another better. This interview will be your first graded assignment." Miss Clements began to scribble a long list of things we needed to find out about our "interviewee" on the board.

When Miss Clements called out names a few minutes later, I stood up, watching as a tiny girl with red, curly hair made her way over to my desk. She wore a long patchwork skirt in different colors and a Care Bear T-shirt. Her hair was bunched into two poufed-out pigtails.

When she stopped at my desk, she did something really weird. She stuck out her hand for me to shake, like we were having a business meeting. "I'm Lydia Applebaum," she said, without the Southern accent everyone else had around here. "Where are you from, Sunflower?"

"Sunny," I said quickly. "I changed my name when I was little."

Lydia shrugged. "Have it your way. If it were me, though, I'd go by Sunflower."

I didn't know how to respond. Lydia didn't notice. She opened her notebook and pulled out a pen with a wiggly blue octopus on top. "Okay, we better get started. Let me guess. You're from up north."

"New Jersey."

"I knew it!" Lydia said with a grin. "I'm pretty good at accents. Why'd you move to North Carolina?"

"Mom's getting her MFA. We're going back home in two years when she finishes her program," I explained to Lydia, even though Mom had told us she was "keeping her options open."

The whole move thing didn't make any sense to me. Mom had told me she needed a change—a break from her job—and the only way she could afford it was if we moved in with my rich grandmother in North Carolina. But Scott could have moved in with us in New Jersey instead of living in his own condo if we needed to cut down on expenses.

When I suggested that to Mom, she just repeated that it was time for a change.

If it were up to Mom, we would stay in North Carolina forever, and I'd barely get to see my dad at all. That's why it was so important to come up with the perfect plan, and soon.

"Master of Fine Arts?" Lydia asked, as if it were something any sixth grader would know.

"In writing. She used to teach junior high, but now she wants to teach college students."

"I want to teach math at Stanford someday." The octopus jiggled as Lydia wrote down everything I said on her paper. "That's where my parents went to school."

I couldn't help wrinkling up my nose. "I hate math."

"I love it. But I love reading and writing, too. And science. I might teach any of those subjects. Or maybe I'll be an environmental lawyer." She looked up at me. "Are you getting all this down?"

I nodded and scribbled some notes. A lawyer would be a good job for Lydia—she sure could talk.

"What about your dad?" she asked. "What's he doing while your mom goes back to school?"

I twisted a piece of hair around my finger. "Um, he owns a bookstore."

"Cool!" Lydia said. "My parents own a health food store. It's called Earthly Goods. Ever heard of it?"

I shook my head. "We just moved here last week."

"Oh, we moved from California at the beginning of the summer so my parents could open the store. This is my first time at a public school. My education will probably suffer, but sometimes you have to make sacrifices."

I gave her a look like *You've got to be kidding.* Who in the world talks like that, anyway?

"Well," Lydia continued, "my parents said Evergreen Middle School'ssupposed to be one of the top schools in the state. But I've been homeschooled all my life by an ex-Stanford professor—my mom—so I'm pretty advanced for my age."

I shrugged. I mean, what else could I say in response to that? I can't stand a bragger.

"So, anyway, you'll have to come out and visit our store at Evergreen Plaza," Lydia said.

"I'm not big on health food."

"We have healthy junk food, too. Like blue corn chips and yummy vegan cookies."

"Vegan cookies?"

"Strictly vegetarian. No eggs or milk or dairy products."

I looked up from my notebook. "You're a vegetarian?"

"Vegan." Lydia threw back her shoulders. "Since I was born."

"Five more minutes," Miss Clements's voice cut through our conversation. "Wrap up your interviews and begin writing your paragraphs."

"All right, we need to hurry up." Lydia glanced at the board and started shooting questions at me lightning fast. "Favorite food?"

"Chocolate chip cookies."

"Mine's fried tofu with peanut sauce."

I made a face, but that didn't stop Lydia. "Favorite activity? Best subject?"

"My favorite activity is art. And my best subject is language arts. I love to write—"

"Well, my best subjects are math, reading, social studies, and science. And my favorite thing to do is write stories and bake vegan desserts and play with my cats."

I was about to ask her about her cats and about why she was a vegan, but before I knew it, Miss Clements called "Time." There was a lot about Lydia that got on my nerves, but I'd discovered we had something in common: we were both animal lovers. And someday, when I was ready, I knew I'd be a vegetarian, too. Lydia wandered back to her desk, and the class went quiet as everyone wrote up their interview paragraphs.

"Miss Clements?" someone called out. "I thought you said we were going to get lockers."

The room started buzzing again, and Miss Clements told us we could finish up our paragraphs for homework. I held my breath, hoping my locker partner would be nice—maybe someone I could be friends with, even if I didn't plan to stick around Evergreen Middle School for long.

"Sunny Beringer and Cassie Evans," Miss Clements called out. A tall girl with long silky hair and tight jean shorts stood up across the room, but she didn't move in my direction.

I walked over to her desk and greeted her with a smile. "Looks like we're locker partners."

Okay, maybe I could have come up with something more original. But, like I always say, there's nothing wrong with stating the obvious when you can't think of anything else. At least I was trying to be friendly.

Cassie didn't smile or respond to what I'd said, and she certainly didn't try to shake my hand either. Instead, she looked me over quickly, then dismissed me with a toss of her hair as we headed down the hall to our locker. I noticed her eyes were rimmed with blue liner and her lips were shining with something that was not Chapstick.

I threw the idea of making friends with my locker partner right out the window. Who wanted to be friends with someone who should have been wearing a shirt that said STUCK-UP AND PROUD OF IT?

I held back a giggle. Madeline would have laughed right along with me.

But as I stared at Cassie's glossy hair fanning out behind her as she rushed down the hall, I found myself running my fingers through my own short hair, wishing I hadn't cut off my ponytail at the beginning of the summer. In June, I had loved riding my bike with Madeline, feeling the warm breeze against my neck without long hair blowing in my eyes. Now the stylish cut had grown out, leaving me with one big shaggy mess, and Mom had been too busy to suggest another trip to the salon.

I'd been too busy, too, until I looked in the mirror this morning. Staring back at me was a short, skinny girl with a mop on her head.

"I'll take the shelf," Cassie decided as we stopped at locker number 312, the first words she spoke to me. Now I'd be stuck throwing my stuff at the bottom. But I didn't argue.

Cassie spun the combination a few times and opened the door like an expert. Then she unzipped her backpack and pulled out all kinds of junk—a mirror, a message board, a poster of some boy with straight teeth and hair that flopped over his forehead. While everyone else stood around practicing opening their locks, Cassie spent the next few minutes decorating.

"Are you sure we're allowed to hang up all that stuff?" I finally asked after she'd Velcroed the mirror and stood in front of it fluffing her hair.

"Why not?" Cassie answered in a tone that suggested I'd asked the stupidest question in the world.

When the bell rang and Miss Clements dismissed us to our next class, I took my whole backpack with me. Since I'd spent the last few minutes in Designer Locker Central instead of practicing, I had no idea if I could get my locker open. I wasn't going to take any chances.

CHAPTER TWO

I got lost on the way to my next two classes and was called "Sunflower" by both of the teachers. I'd fallen into a first-day pattern I was determined to break.

The best part about my morning was third period art. Ms. Rusgo was the only person besides Lydia who looked disappointed when I told her my name was Sunny, not Sunflower.

"I'm sorry to hear that." Her bracelets jangled on her wrist as she made a note on the roll. "I think Sunflower is a fabulous name. Wish I'd been given a cool name like that," she said in a dreamy voice.

I didn't know what to make of my art teacher with her multicolored dress, long flowing hair, and musical voice, but I couldn't stop staring at her, and it didn't take her long to weave her spell over the rest of the class either.

"The key to creating meaningful art," Ms. Rusgo told us as she passed out sheets of paper with a heart outline, "is to harness your inner imagination. Your assignment is to fill in your hearts with colors and images that reflect your true self."

"You mean we should draw things we like to do?" a boy in front of me called out.

"What you fill up your heart with is totally up to you. If I give you too many directions to follow, you won't feel free to create. Dig deep. Dream big. And most importantly, don't run away from your feelings."

Someone in the back of the room snorted. Ms. Rusgo immediately headed in that direction, and soon the room was quiet except for the soft sound of guitar music she'd pulled up on Pandora that was now playing over the speakers. I picked up an oil pastel and watched as my heart filled with overlapping swirls of blue, purple, and green, leaving a heart-shaped space in the middle for a sketch of what mattered most: Mom, Dad, Autumn, and me. Together, not separated by miles and states and tons of unanswered questions.

"You're really good," the girl next to me whispered. I glanced up, noticing her for the first time. She looked like she could be a TV star with her smooth blonde hair, cute flowered shirt, and dimples that showed up when she smiled.

"Thanks," I whispered back, glancing at her drawing. Her heart was filled with flowers and peace signs and smiley faces. "I like yours, too," I told her, even though I didn't think she understood what Ms. Rusgo had meant when she said to "dig deep."

"I'm Jessie," the girl said.

"Sunny."

"I know."

I got the feeling Jessie was someone who didn't miss much, and she had a confidence about her. She was probably one of those popular girls everyone flocked to. But she'd been friendly enough to me, even with my shaggy haircut and my New Jersey accent. I liked her right away.

When the bell rang after third period, Jessie disappeared into the swarm of kids bumping and shoving their way out of the classroom, hurrying to get to the cafeteria. Watching my classroom empty out, I realized that finding my way to class was one thing; figuring out where to sit at lunch was going to be a much bigger problem. I hung back for a few minutes, trying to get my courage up to face a crowded lunchroom.

"Beautiful!" Ms. Rusgo said when she noticed my drawing. "It looks like I have a real artist in my class!"

"Thanks." I looked down at my drawing, pleased with the way the mix of greens and blues captured the loneliness, longing, and worry that I was feeling inside. Art had always been an escape for me, and I could tell Ms. Rusgo was going to be a good teacher. I gave her a quick smile, then grabbed my notebook and pen along with my lunch bag and followed the noisy group of kids down the hall.

A blast of warm air and the smell of cabbage greeted me as I walked into the cafeteria. *Yuck!* The good feeling I'd carried with me since I left Ms. Rusgo slipped away. I scanned the room, searching for a place to sit.

I spotted Jessie right away. She sat at the front with a large group that included Cassie, wouldn't you know? They were smiling and laughing and all chatty-chatty, as if they'd known each other all their lives. Which they probably had.

I paused, noticing an empty seat. Jessie glanced at me for a second, but when she didn't wave me over, I walked away, passing other tables full of kids who were too busy talking to notice me. My stomach clenched and at that moment I felt something I'd never felt before: I was an outsider. A stranger in a middle school full of kids who all seemed to know one another.

Frantically, I searched the cafeteria for a girl with poufed-out pigtails and a patchwork skirt, but I didn't see Lydia anywhere. Sitting with a bragger would have been better than sitting by myself. But when I didn't spot her, I made my way to the back of the cafeteria, where I found an almost-empty table.

A small boy wearing glasses sat at one end, nibbling on a sandwich, his nose in a book. His ears stuck out and his hair stuck up. He looked like a mad scientist. "Hi," I said as I sank down onto a chair.

He glanced up from his book, which had dragons on the front. For a minute, he looked like he'd forgotten he was in the cafeteria.

"What are you reading?" I asked.

"*Scallingworth's Lair,*" the boy said, pointing to the cover. "Book three."

"I like fantasy, too," I told him.

He nodded, then turned back to his dragons. *So much for conversation.*

I sighed and opened my sketchbook. The boy wasn't into talking, but at least he hadn't told me I couldn't sit at his table. I was in uncharted territory, and I had to take what I could get.

I turned to a fresh page and drew our house the way it had looked when we left last week: my favorite climbing tree in the front yard, where I'd tied a blue and green scarf on a high branch years ago; the front porch that sagged in the middle, and the mismatched pillows scattered on the old porch swing; the paint peeling off the shutters Scott had made himself, carving out moons and stars at the tops.

I paused and closed my eyes, replaying our last moments together.

"It's going to be okay," Scott had said after he explained why I couldn't stay with him at his condo: he was too busy running his store and going back to school to take care of an eleven-year-old and, besides, Mom would never leave me behind.

I wanted to shake him by the shoulders and yell, "How can you just let us go?" Instead, I noticed the way his face looked older, like he hadn't slept well in weeks. I stared into Scott's blue-green eyes, swallowing over the apple-sized lump in my throat. "I'm going to miss you so much," I whispered.

"Not as much as I'm going to miss you, Sunflower," he said, and then everything started happening so fast I couldn't slow it down. Mom and Autumn threw the last of the bags into the trunk. Everyone said their goodbyes again.

I remembered the way Scott stood out front waving, while Stellaluna, my perfect little black cat, wrapped herself around his legs. As we pulled out of the driveway and took off down the street, Scott and Stellaluna got smaller and smaller . . . until I couldn't see them at all.

I opened my eyes, staring down at my drawing of home. I couldn't bring myself to sketch in Scott and Stellaluna.

Luckily, the bell rang, and I snapped my sketchbook shut, trying to block those last images from my mind. I jumped up and joined the wave of students exiting the cafeteria, determined to be on time for the rest of my classes and to let all my other teachers know my name before they could call me Sunflower.

And it worked.

CHAPTER THREE

Mom had an appointment and didn't come back to the house until Autumn and I were setting the table with my grandmother's everyday dishes—crystal glasses and china fancier than any we'd ever used back in New Jersey. "Hi, girls!" she said, dropping her bag full of books on the counter. "How was your first day of school?"

"Great!" Autumn said. She was launching into all the stuff she'd already told me about how super-awesome third grade was at her new school when Grandma Grace entered the room.

"Shoes off, girls," she interrupted. "I just had my floors done last week, remember?"

"Sorry, Grandma," Autumn mumbled as the two of us pulled off our shoes, dropping them in the box Grandma Grace had left at the entranceway.

"And Rebecca, please hang your things on the hook or take them up to the office," Grandma Grace continued. "I like to keep my countertops uncluttered."

"Got it," Mom said, disappearing upstairs. I wondered how she felt, being bossed around by her mother after living on her own for years. It's not like I minded the No Shoes rule since I spent a lot of time barefoot anyway; it was more about the fact that we were now living in someone else's house, and we had to do whatever she said.

One thing I knew for sure: Grandma Grace's big white house with the black shutters and the wraparound porch would never feel like home to me.

When we sat down at the long, shiny table a few minutes later, Mom at one end and Grandma Grace at the other, Autumn started talking about school again. A chandelier sparkled above us. I closed my eyes for a second and pictured home: comfortable chairs around a kitchen table set with mismatched dishes and plastic glasses, Scott in his seat across from me, Stellaluna rubbing against my ankles. Even though he didn't live with us, Scott was always there for dinner. He was usually the one cooking since, most of the time, Mom had late meetings or errands to run after work.

"What about you, Sunny?" Mom asked, snapping me out of my daydream. "How do you like middle school?"

"It's just like I thought it was going to be. Perfectly awful."

Everyone stared at me. It was like I'd knocked over my water glass on purpose, and it had splashed on top of all the food on the table. "Oh, honey." Mom put her hand on top of mine. "It can't be that bad."

"Yes, it is," I said. "I got lost a million times. I didn't get a chance to practice opening my locker because my locker partner is a snob. All the teachers are mean. And everyone made fun of my name. You must have named me *Sunflower* as a punishment."

"I named you Sunflower because sunflowers stand tall and proud."

"Well, I'm short."

"I said they *stand* tall. Height doesn't have anything to do with it. Besides, they're the sort of flowers everyone notices."

"Who wants to be noticed? I don't like being stared at."

Mom laughed. I didn't get what was so funny. I looked over at her. Did she have the name already picked out before she adopted me because she'd always wanted an unusual name? Or did she take one look at me and imagine that someday I'd do something that people all over the world would recognize me for, so I needed a bold name to stand out?

"So," Mom said, "why didn't you just tell everyone your name was Sunny?"

"I did, but you were *supposed* to change my name on my records."

"I'm sorry," Mom said. "I thought they'd taken care of it."

"Well, they didn't, which really stinks. Plus, I've already got tons of homework and it's only the first day."

"We don't have any homework," Autumn said in a sing-song voice. "Miss Denton said she's giving us a break for the first week."

I shot her a dirty look.

"Middle school takes some time to get used to." Grandma Grace ran a hand over her smooth, silvery hair, which didn't have a strand out of place. She was still wearing the matching tennis skirt and top she'd worn to the Club that afternoon. "Evergreen is one of the best schools in the state."

I didn't reply. Being the best middle school in the state didn't mean kids were friendly or teachers were understanding. It just meant you worked harder.

"I'm sure it can't be that bad," Mom said. "There must be some nice kids."

"Everyone already knows everyone. There are three elementary schools that feed into Evergreen, so all the kids already have a group of friends. Except me."

"I can't believe you're the only new student in the entire sixth grade," Mom stated.

I shrugged and looked down at my mashed potatoes, coleslaw, and fried chicken. I inhaled the delicious aroma and wondered what Lydia would have to say if she was eating with us. "There is one other new girl who's from California. We had to interview each other in language arts."

"See?" Mom's face lit up. "I knew you couldn't be the only new student. What's she like?"

"She's not someone I'd ever be friends with. She's been homeschooled all her life and she thinks she's a genius or something." Lydia may actually be a genius, for all I know. But that doesn't mean she has to brag about it.

"Beggars can't be choosers," Grandma Grace said, and Autumn giggled.

"What's that supposed to mean?" I asked.

"It means you shouldn't be so quick to judge," Mom answered, instead. "She's new and you're new, so maybe you'll become friends."

"Yeah, right," I mumbled.

"Why did her family move all the way from California?" Mom asked.

"They opened a health food store. They must have too many out in California."

Grandma Grace put down her fork. "You say they moved here recently? What's the name of this health food store?"

"I can't remember," I said. "It's a vegetarian store."

Grandma Grace frowned. "Vegetarian?"

"Yup. Lydia's been vegan all her life."

"Hmm . . . I think they may have opened that new shop in our strip mall."

"Maybe," I said, though I didn't think they'd ever run into each other. Grandma Grace owns Luxury Furs and Leathers, a place I planned to spend very little time in, and I was sure Lydia would stay away from it altogether. I still had no idea how my grandmother and I were supposed to get along—an animal-lover like me and a lady who sold the furs of dead animals in her store.

"Well, *I* made a new friend today," Autumn said, changing the subject. "Her name's Hallie and she has a pet hedgehog and she's really good at the monkey bars. Can she come over after school tomorrow?"

Mom smiled. While Autumn spent the rest of dinner talking about her new friend, thoughts began churning in my mind. Maybe I didn't have the solution yet, but two years of being a member of Scott's Odyssey of the Mind team had taught me that thinking outside the box always started with a lot of brainstorming. But if I didn't get started soon, I could get stuck in Bennetsville for good.

After I helped with the dishes, I raced upstairs, closing the door behind me.

I pulled out my notebook and wrote at the top: "Sunny's Super-Stupendous Plan to Get Mom and Dad Back Together."

When Mom had told us we were moving away, I'd asked if she was breaking up with Scott.

"It's good for people to have time apart," Mom said. "Let's look at this as an adventure. We'll see what happens."

"What kind of adventure?" I'd asked, but what I really wanted to know was *An adventure where you date other people?*

Mom didn't give me any more details. She was an expert at answering my questions without actually ever answering them.

Which only left me wondering what, exactly, was going on between Mom and Scott?

I'd watched enough Disney movies to learn that if you're lovesick, the only cure is to be with the one you love. But Mom didn't act like someone with a broken heart. She'd completely forgotten she was in love. And, apparently, Scott had forgotten, too.

Now it was up to me to remind them.

I brainstormed without stopping to cross out ideas that sounded ridiculous or too out-there because you never knew if something was going to work until you actually tried it. And I needed lots of possibilities to solve a problem as big and important as this one.

I'm not sure how long I sat there on the bed, legs tucked beneath me, scribbling away in my notebook. When I was done, I read back over my list and smiled. Then I jumped up from the bed. It was time to get started.

I dug through my drawer full of photos until I found my favorites: the whole family in front of our tent on a camping trip; Scott and me on the porch swing; Scott, Autumn, and me building a sandcastle at the beach. They'd be perfect for the refrigerator. I found a few more family shots from different holidays—Easter, Christmas, Halloween. I could stick those in little frames and put them on the computer desk where Mom always sat when she was working.

I picked up a photo of Scott leaning against the big oak tree in our yard. He looked like a movie star with his hair all ruffled from the wind, a lock of it falling over his forehead. He wasn't wearing his glasses so you could gaze into his deep-blue eyes. It was exactly the kind of picture that belonged on a bathroom mirror.

But the best idea I'd come up with, number five on the list, would have to wait for the weekend. I opened my laptop and clicked on a YouTube video that showed how to make a beautiful vase.

When Saturday came around, I'd be ready.

SUNNY'S SUPER-STUPENDOUS PLAN TO GET MOM AND DAD BACK TOGETHER

1. Tell Scott that Mom has heavy bags under her eyes from crying so much, and to please send the Eezy Breezy Sleep Mask or a pound of cucumbers.

2. Ask Mom to send Scott a pair of suspenders. Tell her that he has already lost four pounds because he's too sad to eat, and his jeans keep falling down.

3. Put up photos of Scott all over the house: on the refrigerator, on Mom's desk, on top of Mom's dresser, and on the bathroom mirror.

4. Find glamorous photos of Mom and send them to Scott.

5. Send flowers to Mom from "A Secret Admirer." This will make Scott jealous enough to change his mind about letting Mom move so far away.

6. Make a playlist of Scott's favorite love songs—the mushier, the better! Be sure to blast it in the house and in the car every time you get in. Make a playlist of Mom's favorite love songs and send it to Scott.

7. Ask Mom to make Scott's Manicotti Special. At the dinner table, take a bite, sigh, and say, "It just doesn't taste the same without Scott here to share it."

8. Ask Mom about the old days, when she and Scott first became boyfriend and girlfriend. Ask Scott the same thing.

9. Bake Mom's special mint Oreo pie and send it to Scott. Put a card inside the box that says, "Made for you, with love from Rebecca."

10. Ask Grandma Grace for a chore list to earn some extra money. Buy a gift certificate for Mom and Scott to a fancy Italian restaurant. Make sure it has candlelight, wine, and spaghetti for two, just like in *Lady and the Tramp*. Give them the gift certificate when Scott comes to visit at Christmas time (or sooner).

11. Enter one of those Perfect Family contests. When Mom and Scott see the winning entry, they'll realize how much they belong together. Not only that, but the whole family wins a trip to Disney World!

12. Enter the "Perfect Husband" contest. Tell all about how Scott would make a perfect husband for Mom and wait for your entry to be published, then show it to Mom. Enter the "Perfect Wife" contest and send the winning published entry to Scott.

CHAPTER FOUR

From: MadelineL@ilovebooks.com
To: sunnykid@CreativityisCool.com
Miss You!!!!!!

Hi Sunny! How's NC? When do u start your new school?
I miss u!

Xoxo, Madeline

From: SunnyKid@CreativityisCool.com
To: MadelineL@ilovebooks.com
Re: Miss You!!!!!

Hi Madeline!

We started school last week. Middle School!!!! Somehow, I survived.

I'm sending you a super-long letter I wrote in the cafeteria. The only other person who sat at my table all week was this boy who had his nose buried in a book about dragons. So I had plenty of time to write letters.

I miss u soooo much!!!!!!! Xoxoxoxoxoxox, Sunny

***

On Friday evening, we called Scott for the first time in almost a week. Mom let us talk to him after the first day of school, then told us we were going to stick with weekly calls from now on.

Both Autumn and I had protested, but Mom said, "Scott's pretty busy between work and classes."

"Yeah, but—" I started to say, but Mom cut me off.

"If anything comes up and you really need to talk to him, of course you can call. But for now, I think it's better to stick to a time when he's expecting us so he'll have time to talk."

"I bet this was your idea," I said. Scott would always make time for us, no matter when we phoned.

Mom raised an eyebrow. "Actually, we both came up with the idea," she said, though I didn't believe her.

At least Mom didn't rush us that night. I raced for the phone and grabbed it before Autumn could, taking it into the den where I closed the door behind me.

"Oh, Sunflower, I'm so sorry," Scott said after I'd filled him in on everything that had happened at school, which means I told him a lot more than I'd told Mom. Mom was already busy with her own classes and her writing and look-ing up old friends. Plus, whenever I told her what was going on, she was all about giving advice. Sometimes I just wanted someone to listen. "So you've been sitting by yourself in the cafeteria all week?"

"Yup. Well, not completely alone. Another boy sits at the table, but he always has his nose in a book."

Scott laughed. "Sounds like me when I was in junior high. Books were a great escape."

"I've been drawing in my sketchbook," I told him. "And writing letters to Madeline."

"There's nothing wrong with that. But you know, Sunny, eventually I did find a group of kids to sit with. Sometimes these things take time."

I didn't need time. What I needed was to get back home, where I already had friends and a dad, too. I felt an ache in my chest and clutched the phone tighter.

"So tell me how the other half lives," Scott said. "Have you hit your head on any chandeliers yet? Broken any crystal goblets?"

I giggled. "Grandma Grace makes us take off our shoes so we won't scuff up her hardwood floors. And you have to be careful when you sit down for dinner that you don't slide right off the shiny chairs—a maid comes every week and polishes the chairs, can you believe that? Mom says Grandma Grace has always been a neatness nut, and she's not giving an inch even though she has three new people living in her house."

"Oh, I can just see it now. How's your mom adjusting to being back in Grandma's house, maid service and all?"

"Actually"—I paused a minute, choosing my words carefully. I had to make this good—"she's miserable. Absolutely miserable. She fights with Grandma Grace all the time. And she's really lonely. I think she cries every night, because her eyes look all swollen in the morning."

"Hmm . . ." Scott hesitated. I guess he was letting those words sink in. I thought about Sunny's Super-Stupendous Plan and remembered to make it dramatic. That was key.

"Do you think you can send one of those Eezy Breezy Sleep Masks so she can sleep better? Or maybe a pound of cucumbers? That will help make the bags under her eyes go away."

"Maybe it's allergies," Scott finally said. "It can be hard getting used to a new part of the country—"

"Oh, it's not allergies. I know loneliness when I see it."

About that time, there was a knock and a bang on the door, and then Autumn threw it open, saying she couldn't wait any longer. So I said my goodbyes and love-yous and handed the phone to my sister.

After Autumn and I finished talking to Scott, Mom got on the phone, but not for long. She told him a little about her classes and asked about his, and before you knew it, she was saying we'd taken up enough of his time and we'd talk to him next week.

It was a normal, polite conversation—the kind you have with someone you see every day. Like, "Can you remember to pick up tomatoes and pickles at the grocery store?"

Mom did not sound like someone who was missing the love of her life. The situation was even more drastic than I'd first suspected.

As soon as Mom hung up, I raced upstairs and pulled out my notebook, where I'd taken notes from the YouTube video. Then I opened my craft supply drawer and pulled out a blue glass bottle, a pile of tissue paper, and a bottle of glue. Now all I had to do was mix up some glue and water and, voila! Instant decoupage.

Using my paintbrush, I glued the tissue paper to the bottle and coated the top of the paper with more decoupage. According to YouTube, I had to apply at least three coats, waiting for each layer to dry before adding another. It took most of the evening, but that worked out fine since I couldn't get started on the rest of the project until everyone was in bed.

I waited until I heard Mom's and Grandma Grace's footsteps on the stairs followed by the shutting of bedroom doors. Fifteen minutes later, I grabbed my strongest pair of scissors, a cloth bag, and my flashlight.

The old wooden steps creaked and my heart thumped as I tiptoed downstairs in the dark. By the time I made it to the back door, the grandfather clock was three minutes away from striking midnight.

I waited until the clock bonged, a loud enough noise to cover up the squeak of the back door. The hairs on my arms rose up as I stepped out into the backyard. I quickly glanced back at the house. Completely black except for a dim light in the kitchen and a hall light on upstairs.

There was no time to waste.

A summer breeze blew through my thin pajamas as I flicked on my flashlight, making me shiver as the dark shadows of tree branches moved against the grass. Luckily, I didn't have to go far. Mrs. Wright's rosebushes lined the back fence of her yard, so all I had to do was open the gate she shared with Grandma Grace.

The rest was easy. Almost. All I can say is there's probably a good reason for using special scissors for gardening. Especially if you don't want to get pricked by thorns. But if you saw away long enough, art scissors will do the trick. I filled my bag with red, white, and pink roses and dashed back across the yard before anyone noticed I was gone.

***

"It's about time!" Autumn called out to me as I came downstairs the next morning. "I thought you were going to sleep all day. I wanted to wake you up but Mom wouldn't let me. Look what we found on the front porch a few minutes ago!"

I yawned, trying to act uninterested in the whole thing. "What's for breakfast?"

"I'll heat up the leftover pancakes," Grandma Grace said.

"Look!" Autumn pointed to the vase full of pink, red, and white roses. "Flowers for Mom. From a Secret Admirer!"

I dropped into a chair and laughed. "A Secret Admirer?"

She shoved the card into my hand. "Read it."

"'To Rebecca,'" I read, though I'd already memorized the words. "'You are as beautiful as a rose, without the thorns. From Your Secret Admirer.'"

"Can you believe it?" Autumn asked with a giggle. "Mom has a secret admirer!"

"I'm not sure why you find that so hard to believe." Mom smiled and handed me a glass of orange juice.

"What do you think Scott will say when he hears about it?" I asked.

"He'll probably get on a plane and fly down here to investigate," Autumn said.

"Investigate?" I repeated.

"Yeah. It means put the clues together, like a detective. We're learning about investigations in science."

I rolled my eyes. "I know what it means, Autumn."

"I bet it's from one of your old flames," Grandma Grace said.

"Doubtful," Mom replied. "Last I heard, James had moved to Canada to protest the United States' war policies. With a lady friend."

"I wasn't talking about James," Grandma Grace said. "I was talking about Doug Simpson."

Mom snorted. "Doug Simpson? I never went out with him."

"I know. But he's had a thing for you since junior high school. He still lives here, you know. Divorced. I ran into him a few weeks ago and mentioned that you were moving back here."

Mom groaned. "I wish you hadn't said anything, Mom."

I clunked my glass down on the table. "James? Doug Simpson?"

"James was my very first boyfriend," Mom said, a dreamy look in her eyes.

Well, this was just ridiculous. Mom had never talked about old boyfriends before.

Autumn giggled. I didn't. "Who's Doug Simpson?" I asked.

Mom rolled her eyes. Then she shook her head and sighed at the same time. "Just some guy I knew growing up."

"Don't write him off so quickly," Grandma Grace said. "People change."

I didn't like the direction this conversation was taking. It wasn't where I needed it to go. "Mom already has Scott, you know. Maybe he's the one who sent the flowers."

My grandmother raised an eyebrow. "He's in New Jersey, and your mother is here. If he wanted to send flowers, don't you think he'd at least sign his name?"

Mom laughed. "Scott is definitely not the type to send flowers. Besides, it's probably just a joke from one of my old friends."

"Think what you want," Grandma Grace said, "but if I were you, I'd keep my eyes peeled."

"I can't wait to tell Scott about this," I said.

"It'll give him a good laugh," Mom said.

I curled my hand in a ball under the table so no one would see the cuts. I wanted Scott to laugh about it as much as I wanted another thorn in my finger.

Romance was turning out to be way more complicated than I thought.

CHAPTER FIVE

From: MadelineL@ilovebooks.com
To: SunnyKid@CreativityisCool.com
My New Teacher!!

We start school on Tuesday! Miss Harkin is staying home
with her baby & I got the new teacher: A MAN! His name's
Mr. Stohler. Emma G. says he's old and bald! Help!!!

From SunnyKid@CreativityisCool.com
To MadelineL@ilovebooks.com
Re: My New Teacher!!

Sorry you didn't get Miss Harkin. When did you talk to
Emma G.? I have three male teachers this year. They aren't
bad, but they aren't great like my art teacher either. One of
them wears ties with smiley faces on them every single day.

From: SunnyKid@CreativityisCool.com
To: Scott@BookBuyers.com
Mom Has a Secret Admirer!

Hi Scott! You'll never believe what we found on the front porch! A vase of roses for Mom, from a secret admirer. The note said: "You are as beautiful as a rose, without the thorns." I think you need to get down here AS SOON AS POSSIBLE to keep an eye on the situation.

Love,
Sunflower

P.S. Mom cries every night, even though she tries to hide it. I'm sure of it now. She must be wishing we had stayed in New Jersey with you! Can you please send that Eezy Breezy Mask or those cucumbers? ASAP!!

From: Scott@BookBuyers.com
To: SunnyKid@CreativityisCool.com
Re: Mom Has a Secret Admirer!

Roses from a secret admirer? Well, your mother is a beautiful woman, you know. I wish I could hop on a plane to come see you, but I can't get away from the store right now.

Promise me you'll keep me posted!

Love,
Scott

***

My weekend was a complete flop. The secret admirer had fallen, *SPLAT!* Scott didn't sound the least bit worried about Mom's ex-boyfriends who might be sending her flowers. And Mom wasn't any better. She'd totally brushed away the idea that the flowers could have been from Scott, and she hadn't said one word about the photos I'd put up all over the house, not even the one on the bathroom mirror!

I needed a new and improved plan, and I needed one super-quick. The longer Mom and Scott were apart, the harder it would be to get them back together.

I spent all weekend revving up my brain power, meditating in one of those tricky lotus positions Mom had taught me. Still, I came up with nothing.

Zero. Zilch.

My creative thinking skills, the ones that had helped our team place third in the regional Odyssey of the Mind competition last year, had flown right out the window. I needed to jumpstart my creativity.

And that's why I found myself jotting down *September 10* in my notebook when there was an announcement about OM tryouts over the intercom on Monday morning, even though I hadn't planned to join any clubs at this new school.

I bit my lip, thinking about how different Odyssey of the Mind would be without Scott as a coach. He'd volunteered for the job the last two years. I pictured him wearing his blue COACH cap, cheering and clapping about team members' ideas, no matter how silly they sounded, because "you never know when a stupid idea is actually a genius one." He'd bounce on his toes, waving his hands in the air to get the rest of us excited as he scribbled everything down on a big chart board, and then he'd say, "You guys are awesome." Instead of high-fiving us, he'd toss us a Jolly Rancher or a chocolate kiss when we shared especially out-of-the-box ideas.

I was still thinking about going out for the team when I sat down next to Jessie in art class that morning. She smiled at me, and I smiled back.

"Today we are going to work on self-portraits," Ms. Rusgo said as she twirled her long hair into a bun and pinned it with chopsticks. "I call this unit 'Window to My Soul.'"

"We're going to draw pictures of ourselves?" Brent called out from the front row. "Cool."

"Actually, we're going to draw representations of ourselves. That means the goal is not to draw a picture that resembles what you look like in the mirror. I want your drawings to reflect what you look like inside."

A wave of murmurs and nervous giggles filled the room.

"Nothing to worry about," Ms. Rusgo said. "I don't want you to focus on accuracy. For example, you don't need to try to make your nose look exactly like the one on your face. I want you to draw 'the real you.'"

A few more giggles rippled through the classroom. Ms. Rusgo ignored them as she passed out large pieces of paper and asked some kids to pass out the oil pastels.

"But Ms. Rusgo, if we're not drawing our faces," someone else called out, "what are we supposed to draw?"

"Aha," Ms. Rusgo said. "That is a good question." She turned to her easel at the front of the room and sketched the outline of a head and shoulders. "It's up to you to decide what you want to put on the inside. And, remember, use your colors wisely—as we discussed last week, colors evoke feelings and memories."

"It's like the heart paintings," Jessie whispered to me. "We can just draw things we like."

I didn't want to disagree with her. I nodded and got to work. Ms. Rusgo turned on her music, and a folk song—one I recognized from Mom's playlist—filled the room. I fell into a sort of trance, like I always do when I'm concentrating on my artwork.

By the time Ms. Rusgo asked everyone to start cleaning up, I'd drawn stars for my eyes, our home in New Jersey as my nose, Stellaluna stretched out for a mouth that only curled up a little on the ends, and Mom and Scott in circles on each side of my mouth, for the cheeks.

Jessie drew in her breath when she saw my paper. "Ooo, I love it!"

"You did a nice job, too," I said, looking at her portrait. It was almost identical to her heart drawing, even though Ms. Rusgo had stopped at our table and suggested that she draw personal things, not the symbols you find on T-shirts and notebooks.

"Thanks," Jessie said. "I wish I was an artist like you."

I felt my cheeks flush and looked back down at my portrait. Jessie's was cheerful and happy, all pinks and yellows and sunshine, as if she'd never had a negative thought enter her head. Mine was full of darkness—blues and grays and shadows.

"Hey, you're new around here, aren't you?" Jessie asked as we put away our supplies. "Where'd you move from?"

"New Jersey."

"I thought so. I have cousins who live there. Every time we visit, we go to the most awesome Italian restaurant, Valencio's. Have you ever heard of it?"

I shook my head. "I love Italian food, though."

She grinned. "Hey, you want to sit with us at lunch today? I just have to stop at my locker."

"Okay," I said calmly, but my heart was doing jumping jacks. Someone had asked me to sit with her at lunch! And not just someone—someone important. Jessie was pretty and friendly, one of the most popular girls in the whole sixth grade. And she had asked me, me, to sit with her.

For a split second, I thought of Dragon Boy. We'd shared a lunch table all last week, me focused on my journal and him on his book. Even though we'd only exchanged a few words, I wondered how he'd feel when I didn't show up today.

After we stopped at Jessie's locker, we headed to the cafeteria. "Hey, ya'll!" Jessie said as we approached her usual table.

"Everyone, this is Sunny. She moved here from New Jersey, and she is the best artist ever."

"Cool," said Chloe Summers, a girl with short white-blonde hair and sparkly earrings who was in my math class. A few of the others looked up at me and waved. But Cassie, my locker partner, didn't wave or smile. She gave me a look that said, *Who do you think you are, trying to make friends with our Jessie?*

I glanced away, quickly sitting down next to Jessie. I was unwrapping my sandwich when I heard my name being called. Or, my ex-name.

"Sunflower, hi!" Lydia ran up to me and dropped her lunch box on the table. "I was looking for you."

"Sunny," I corrected her. My cheeks were blazing. Last week, I'd been so lonely, I would have been thrilled to see Lydia, even if she was a big know-it-all. But now I didn't know how to react.

The other girls stared at Lydia's long skirt, bushy pigtails, and T-shirt that said IF YOU LOVE ANIMALS CALLED PETS, WHY DO YOU EAT ANIMALS CALLED DINNER?

Lydia plopped herself down across from me and started talking like she hadn't even noticed the table was full of people. "So I wanted to tell you that I really liked the poem you read today. It's one of my favorites, too."

"Oh, thanks." Miss Clements had chosen me to read the daily poem. I'd flipped through her collection and picked one of my favorites: "The Road Not Taken," by Robert Frost.

"Oh, I just love Robert Frost! His poems are really deep. Last year, my mom and I did an entire unit on him: symbolism, analysis, metaphors . . ."

I nodded, looking down at my cheese sandwich. The rest of the table had gone eerily silent as the other girls stared at Lydia. Jessie's table was Invitation Only, something I'd figured out on the first day of school.

Lydia pulled out her lunch. "It's a little hard getting used to public school. Mom used to let me decide on my units, and now there's other people telling me what to read and what activities to do. It's definitely not as stimulating, but Mom says I'll get used to it." She unwrapped her sandwich and a strange smell floated up into the air. Then she took a big bite. Tomato sauce oozed out and a slimy brown glob dropped onto her foil.

"Eww!" Cassie screeched. "What is that gross stuff she's eating?"

Lydia put down her sandwich and stood up. She reached across the table to shake Cassie's hand. "I'm Lydia." Cassie gave her a rude look and crossed her arms in front of her chest. That didn't discourage Lydia. "Lydia Applebaum. We're in the same language arts class."

"Whatever," Cassie said. "What in the world is that *thing*?" She wrinkled up her nose and pointed at Lydia's lunch.

Lydia sat back down in her chair and held up her sandwich. "It's a ratatouille sub. Want a bite?"

"Eww, gross!" Cassie said, and some of the other girls echoed her.

Jessie raised an eyebrow. "What's rat-a-too-ee?"

"Grilled eggplant smothered in tomato sauce, spices, and cooked onions."

More Ewws, and this time Jessie joined the chorus.

My stomach clenched as I slid back in my seat. I didn't want to be rude like the rest of the girls, but Lydia's sandwich did look disgusting, and smelled even worse. It reminded me of the eggplant parmigiana Grandma Grace served us on our first night in Bennetsville. That dinner almost made me puke.

Lydia turned toward me. "Would you like to try some?"

I shook my head. "No, thanks."

Chloe plugged her nose. "I can't stand the smell," she said to the girl sitting next to her. "Scoot over!"

"It's really not so bad," Lydia said. "And you never know if you like something until you try it—"

"Forget it." Cassie stood up and grabbed her tray. "I think it's time to find a new place to sit."

"Wait for me!" Chloe said, shooting Lydia a dirty look as she picked up her lunch bag.

Lydia shrugged. "It's better than what you're eating— dead chicken fried and battered? No, thanks."

Jessie narrowed her eyes. "Who invited you to sit at our table anyway?" she shot at Lydia, as the other girls rose to leave the table so quickly it was like the fire alarm had gone off. She turned to me. "You coming, Sunny?"

I glanced over at Lydia. She met my gaze for a second, long enough for me to see hurt in her eyes. Her shoulders slumped as she turned back to her ratatouille sub and took another bite. Like she didn't care if I left or not.

But I knew better.

I glanced back at Jessie. "Come on," she said to me.

For a whole week, I'd been sitting at a table with a boy who didn't even notice I existed. Now I was being asked to sit with one of the most popular girls in sixth grade.

I looked at Lydia a second longer, then, before I could think about it more, I picked up my lunch and took off after Jessie, without looking back.

My stomach hurt for the rest of the day.

SUNNY'S SUPER-STUPENDOUS PLAN TO GET MOM AND DAD BACK TOGETHER

1. Tell Scott that Mom has heavy bags under her eyes from crying so much, and to please send the Eezy Breezy Sleep Mask or a pound of cucumbers. Hasn't sent anything yet.

2. Ask Mom to send Scott a pair of suspenders. Tell her that he has already lost four pounds because he's too sad to eat, and his jeans keep falling down. Mom laughed when I told her this. She said, "Don't you worry. Scott knows how to take care of himself. I bet he's living it up, eating at a different restaurant every night. Gained four pounds is probably more like it!"

3. Put up photos of Scott all over the house: on the refrigerator, on Mom's desk, on top of Mom's dresser, and on the bathroom mirror. Mom is too busy to notice. I asked her if she saw the photo on the bathroom mirror. She didn't even look up from her laptop. Just said, "Mmm-hmm," and kept right on typing.

4. Find glamorous photos of Mom and send them to Scott. Haven't found any yet. Mom is wearing old jeans with her hair pulled back in all the

photos I've looked at. Will have to think about this one more.

5. Send flowers to Mom from "A Secret Admirer." This will make Scott jealous enough to change his mind about letting Mom move so far away. It made Mom start talking about old boyfriends, which was totally disgusting. And Scott just laughed about the whole thing. UGH.

6. Make a playlist of Scott's favorite love songs—the mushier, the better! Be sure to blast it in the house and in the car every time you get in. Make a playlist of Mom's favorite love songs and send it to Scott. Time to get started on this one.

7. Ask Mom to make Scott's Manicotti Special. At the table, take a bite, sigh, and say, "It just doesn't taste the same without Scott here to share it." Mom's too busy with classes. Grandma Grace does most of the cooking. Maybe I should cook it?

8. Ask Mom about the old days, when she and Scott first became boyfriend and girlfriend. Ask Scott the same thing. Haven't gotten around to it yet!

9. ~~Bake Mom's special mint Oreo pie and send it to Scott. Put a card inside the box that says "Made for you, with love from Rebecca."~~ How do you send ice cream pie through the mail?

10. Ask Grandma Grace for a chore list to earn some extra money. Buy a gift certificate for Mom and Scott to a fancy Italian restaurant. Make sure it has candlelight, wine, and spaghetti for two, just like in *Lady and the Tramp*. Give them the gift certificate when Scott comes to visit at Christmas time (or sooner). Haven't asked Grandma Grace yet—she doesn't seem like the type who will actually pay me for chores.

11. Enter one of those Perfect Family contests. When Mom and Scott see the winning entry, they'll realize how much they belong together. Not only that, but the whole family wins a trip to Disney World! Looked in Grandma Grace's magazines but I haven't seen any contest listings.

12. ~~Enter the "Perfect Husband" contest. Tell all about how Scott would make a perfect husband for Mom and wait for your entry to be published, then show it to Mom. Enter the "Perfect Wife" contest and send the winning published entry to Scott.~~ I've been looking for this kind of contest and all I can find is one called "The Perfect Man" or "The Perfect Woman." The winner gets to pick the eligible bachelor or bachelorette of his choice.

TIME FOR SOME NEW IDEAS!!!

CHAPTER SIX

On September tenth, I headed to the Media Center after school for the Odyssey of the Mind tryouts. Sunny's Super-Stupendous Plan had completely stalled. My creative thinking skills were in desperate need of a boost.

I pulled open the door to the center. Kids were crowded around three big tables. My heart dropped to my toenails.

I hesitated in the doorway, thinking back to the conversation I'd had with Scott on the phone that weekend. "I wish you could be my coach," I'd told him. "You're the best coach in the whole world."

There was a long silence on the other end. Scott finally cleared his throat. His voice was a little husky when he spoke. "I wish I could be your coach, too, Sunflower. I'm sure . . . that your new coach will be just as good."

"Excuse me," someone said behind me. I turned around to see Dragon Boy. He gave me a quick smile, then made his way past me. I looked around the room for an empty seat and spotted Lydia. She looked up at me, but didn't wave or yell out, "Sunflower!"

Not that I expected her to.

Instead of giving Lydia a chance, for the last week and a half I'd been sitting with a bunch of girls who mostly ignored me. Cassie hadn't said a word to me yet, and the girls talked about people and things I didn't know anything about. But Jessie always smiled and said hi when I sat down at their table as if she wanted me to be there. So I stayed.

I'm not a horrible person, I told myself every time I remembered Lydia's face as I walked away from her. I tried to think up reasons not to blame myself for what happened. Lydia should have asked if she could sit at the table. She didn't have to bring something smelly and she shouldn't have made rude comments about the other girls' food.

No matter what I told myself, though, the gnawing feeling didn't go away. I always tried to treat people the way I wanted to be treated, and making up excuses didn't take away from the facts. Plain and simple, I'd been mean to Lydia Applebaum.

Every day after language arts, I tried to catch up to her and apologize, but by the time I made it to the other side of the room, she was out the door and we didn't have any other classes together. And now, here we were at the media center, both of us attempting to get a spot on the Odyssey of the Mind team.

Well, this is certainly an awkward situation, I thought as I made my way to a seat at the end of the table. A few minutes later, the librarian introduced us to the two team coaches, Coach Baker and Coach Alanah. "Up to seven members will be chosen for each team," Mrs. Rodriguez said. "OM members from last year will be given automatic spots if they can prove themselves at tryouts. How many of you were on the team last year?"

I glanced around the room. Great. Seven hands in the air, which meant only seven spots for new team members.

"Evergreen prides itself on presenting an impressive Odyssey of the Mind team," Mrs. Rodriguez continued. "As some of you know, both of last year's teams made it all the way to Worlds!"

Cheers, claps, and hoots filled the room.

"We have a reputation to live up to. Anyone who makes the team must be committed to after-school practices as well as meeting on the weekends. You must be dedicated to hard work, creative expression, thinking outside the box, and most importantly—" She paused and nodded at us.

"*Teamwork!*" some of the kids yelled.

"Okay, Coach Baker and Coach Alanah, take it away!" She smiled at us. "Evergreen's expecting great things from you this year."

The coaches started with a short explanation of how students needed to prepare for the OM competition in March: Two-thirds of the score would come from preparing an eight-minute skit with scenery, costumes, and sets. One-third of the score was based on responding to a spontaneous problem, which we wouldn't know until the competition. For tryouts, the coaches split us into groups, and the next half hour flew by as we worked on spontaneous problems: Come up with a clever name for someone working in a specific occupation. That was an easy one: Ima Reader for a bookstore owner. And animal rhymes: an antelope ate my cantaloupe.

After we'd finished the rounds of verbal problems, Coach Baker announced it was time for a hands-on problem. "You'll work in pairs to make the longest construction between two desks using toothpicks, paper, and clay."

Before I knew it, Coach Baker was calling out my name with Lydia's. I'd been handed the perfect opportunity to apologize for abandoning her at the lunch table, but when I looked over, she was glaring at me.

This wasn't going to be easy.

When the coach finished giving instructions, Lydia and I walked over to the supply table together. I was about to tell her I was sorry when she said, "They're snobs. S-N-O-B-S. I wouldn't waste my time with them if I were you."

My apology melted right into my tongue. No way was I admitting that maybe she was right about them. "Jessie's nice," I said as I picked up a box of toothpicks. "We're in art class together. She's the one who asked me to sit with her that day, and I told her I would."

"Uh-huh," Lydia said. I followed her to a back table and we began flattening out the clay.

"It's true," I said. "I don't really know the other girls, but I like Jessie."

"Yeah, she seemed real nice when she was making fun of my lunch."

"Oh, come on. You've got to admit ratatouille looks a little different from what everyone else was eating—"

"What's wrong with being different? That's the problem with those girls. They dress and think and act alike. Boring. Besides, I'm not sure how you can call Jessie 'nice.' Leaving someone at a table by herself is not nice." From the way Lydia was staring at me I knew she wasn't just talking about Jessie and her crowd.

I bit my lip. I was a terrible, rotten person. "Look, Lydia, about what happened—"

"Forget it," she said, brushing off my apology before I could get the words out. "All I'm saying is, who wants to be friends with people like that anyway? Who needs them?"

I shrugged and looked down at the clay.

"Four minutes!" Coach Baker announced.

"Come on," Lydia said. "We have to hurry."

"I'm not the one wasting time."

Lydia glared at me, but then she got busy. We worked in silence, somehow finding a rhythm. Our clay chain ended up being the longest in the room.

"Awesome job, girls!" Coach Baker said, giving us both high fives. "Now you can high-five each other. It's all about teamwork, you know."

Lydia looked down at her hands, then wiped them on her skirt before walking back to her seat. I guess she had finally gotten her chance to walk away from me.

I dropped down into my chair, trying not to think about her as the coach showed us our last problem. He held up a photo of a wedding day: a bride in a long white gown and veil, a groom in a tuxedo, the cake between them. "You have two minutes to come up with a caption for this photo. And . . . go!"

Everyone around me began scribbling wildly. I sat there, paralyzed. As soon as I looked at the photo, it hit me: I'd never seen Mom and Scott gazing at each other the way the bride and groom were staring at each other in the picture. Had I forgotten because it had been such a long time and things had changed between them?

"Time!" Coach Baker called out. I looked down at my blank sheet of paper. I was doomed.

CHAPTER SEVEN

From: SunnyKid@CreativityisCool.com
To: MadelineL@ilovebooks.com
Odyssey of the Mind Tryouts

I think I blew the Odyssey of the Mind tryouts. I wish I was home and we could be on the same team together, like always. What do you think of sixth grade so far? How's your new teacher?

((Hugs)) Sunny

From: MadelineL@ilovebooks.com
To: SunnyKid@CreativityisCool.com
Re: Odyssey of the Mind Tryouts

I'm sure you did fine at the tryouts! You always come up with the greatest ideas.

Sixth grade is going to be pretty good. Mr. S isn't old and bald! He's always saying, "All right? Cool." And he likes to high-five people all the time. Carmen Santelli has a crush on him! She's already told half the girls she thinks he's cute!

((Hugs)) Madeline

From: SunnyKid@CreativityisCool.com
To: Scott@BookBuyers.com
Cukes

We didn't get any cucumbers yet. Mom could sure use them.

From: Scott@BookBuyers.com
To: SunnyKid@CreativityisCool.com
Re: Cukes

The cucumbers are on the way! I picked up your favorite Kirby cukes at the farmer's market last week. I also sent a jar of that Green Goddess salad dressing that you love.

***

"You will never believe what happened to me today," Grandma Grace said as we sat down for dinner that night.

"What, Grandma?" Autumn asked. "Did a famous person come to your shop?"

"Famous isn't exactly the word I'd use." Grandma Grace turned to me. "I believe your friend's mother paid me a visit today."

My eyes opened wide.

"You know, the one who owns the health food store. She marched right into my shop carrying a plate full of vegan cookies."

"That was nice of her," Mom said.

"Did you bring home the cookies?" Autumn asked.

Grandma Grace shook her head. "I threw them in the trash."

"Oh, come on, Mom," my mother said. "Just because they're vegan doesn't mean they taste bad."

"It had nothing to do with that. It had to do with this." Grandma Grace got up and pulled something out of her pocketbook, then slammed it down on the table.

I reached for the pamphlet and read the words to myself silently. *These babies have lost their mama. Are you wearing her on your back?*

"Awww," Autumn said. "They're so cute. Let me see!"

I stared at the photo of the raccoon and her babies, unable to look away.

"Wow." Mom took the pamphlet and studied it. "Looks like someone doesn't like the fact that you're selling furs."

"What gives her the right?" Grandma Grace snatched the pamphlet from Mom's hands. "If she doesn't want to wear a fur coat, she doesn't have to. But she has a lot of nerve sneaking her inflammatory pamphlet under a plate of so-called cookies."

"I think it's a pretty creative way to get her message across," Mom said. "Did you at least take a look at it?"

"Why would I want to read a bunch of propaganda?" Grandma Grace snapped, her cheeks turning pink. "I've heard of these animal rights fanatics. They're nothing but trouble. And now I have one just a few doors down from my store!"

"But—but you're not hurting animals, are you, Grandma Grace?" Autumn asked.

"Of course not," Grandma Grace said. "All I'm doing is buying coats from a supplier, coats that make people feel warm and happy."

I swallowed over the lump in my throat. I wanted to speak up, but I couldn't get the words out.

"Well," Mom said, glancing at me and then back at my grandmother, "not everyone would agree with your point of view." She cleared her throat, like she was trying to keep herself from saying something that would start an argument.

"It's one thing to come right out and oppose my business," Grandma Grace said. "It's another, Rebecca, to come in posing as a friendly neighbor, and to hide *this*"—she waved the pamphlet in the air—"under an innocent plate of cookies!"

Mom pursed her lips. I could tell she was trying hard to keep her words inside, same as I was. She'd told me how she'd argued with my grandmother when she first announced her plans to open the store ten years ago, but their relationship was already on "strained terms." "She wasn't about to listen to *me*," Mom had said.

I watched my mom now, the way she concentrated hard on spearing a green bean on her plate, then wiped her mouth with a napkin. If Mom and Grandma Grace had been getting along better back then, could she have convinced her to open a different shop, one that didn't sell fur coats?

"So," Mom said, "you think this lady, the one who came into your store, is the mother of Sunny's new friend?"

"She's not my friend," I said quickly. "I mean, she's in my language arts class, that's all."

"It's certainly a coincidence," Grandma Grace said. "This girl says her parents just opened a health food store. How many health food stores have opened in Bennetsville recently?"

"You should ask her," Autumn said, turning to me. "Ask her if her mom's the one who made Grandma Grace upset."

Silence fell over the table. Grandma Grace stomped over to the trash can and tossed in the pamphlet. Then she sat down and refilled her glass of tea. After a long sip, she said, "Well, enough about that." She waved her hand like she was trying to push Lydia and her family's health food store right off the map. "So, girls," she said, looking from me to Autumn. "Tell me how things are going at school."

Her words nearly knocked me off my chair. My grandmother never asked about our days. Mom was usually the one talking about us, like "Sunny won the fourth-grade art contest this year for her drawing of a shoe." But here my grandmother was, leaning forward and looking at us . . . with interest.

Autumn jumped right in. "We're learning about body systems in science. Today we made a skeleton out of macaroni."

My sister chattered on and on, but I was still thinking about Luxury Furs. I offered to clean up the kitchen and once everyone had left, I went straight over to the trash can. Slipping my hand inside, I pulled out the pamphlet, brushed off the dirt and crumbs, and stuck it in my back pocket.

When I went up to my room a little while later, I sat down at my desk and began to read.

My eyes scanned the first subtitle: THE MAKING OF FURS—A VERY UGLY BUSINESS.

The suffering of up to 120 animals is sewn into every fur coat.

I bit my lip and looked away from the photo. My grandmother had thrown out the pamphlet without even reading it. Didn't she wonder why people were protesting her business? Or was she really some kind of Cruella de Vil who didn't care what happened to the animals before they were turned into the fur coats that hung in her store?

I swallowed and turned my attention back to the pamphlet. I forced myself to read the front, inside, and back. It was worse than I'd ever imagined. By the time I was done, I knew all about how animals were trapped, how they spent their lives in cages, and how they were killed in horrible ways to make sure no blood showed up on the luxurious fur coats.

I folded my arms on my desk and dropped my head on top of them. I couldn't understand how my grandmother could make her living from an industry that tortured animals. What kind of person was she?

I closed my eyes tight, trying to block out the images. But the words were already stuck in my brain and there was nothing I could do to make them go away.

***

I tried to work on my math homework, but I couldn't concentrate. Before I knew it, I'd raced down to the kitchen, grabbed the phone off the counter, and was dialing Scott's number, even though it wasn't our official night to talk.

I held the phone tight to my ear, listening to it ring and ring. Usually Scott picked up right away. But usually he was expecting our call.

"Hello?"

I could barely make out his voice over all the background noise. "It's me, Sunny," I said a little louder. "Where are you?"

"Is everything okay?"

"Fine. Why is it so noisy? I can hardly hear you!"

"Just a minute, okay?"

There was a pause, and the background noise got quieter. He must have walked to another spot because I could hear him better now. "Sorry about that, Sunny."

"Where are you?" I asked again.

"I'm at Thomas Street Restaurant," Scott said.

I couldn't believe it—Scott was out having fun at a noisy restaurant while I'd been stuck at Grandma Grace's fancy dining room table, listening to her complain about crazy animal rights fanatics. "Who are you having dinner with?"

"Just some friends."

"Who?"

"You don't know them. Some friends from school."

I didn't say anything. I wondered if any of them were female, but I didn't dare ask.

"So, what's up? I didn't expect a call from you on a Wednesday night."

"Oh. Yeah. Sorry to bother you—"

"It's no bother. Did something happen at school today?"

I shook my head but, of course, he couldn't see me over the phone. Scott was so busy with work and school and hanging out with new *friends* that he'd forgotten all about my OM tryouts. He used to give up afternoons and weekends to coach my team, was totally involved from brainstorming to hauling around materials in his truck to giving us hugs and free pizza . . . and now he didn't even ask about tryouts!

It was the first time Scott hadn't been there for me. And I didn't just mean in the same place. He always knew when I needed to talk about something, but tonight it suddenly felt as if we were so . . . distant.

I wanted to tell him I needed a hug. But, at the same time, I felt anger building up inside me, like the water boiling inside a teakettle. Scott had let Mom take us away without even putting up a fight. Didn't he care about us at all?

"Is everything okay with your classes?" Scott asked.

"Yeah."

"How's your new friend—Jessie, was it?"

"She's good."

"And how about your grandma? She's not giving you any trouble, is she?"

"Well, Grandma Grace was all steamed up today. Lydia's mom—Lydia's parents are the ones who own the health food store—brought grandma a plate of vegan cookies with an animal rights pamphlet hidden underneath! It was horrible. You won't believe what they do to animals before they turn them into fur coats. And Grandma thinks the Applebaums are going to cause a lot of trouble, but she deserves it—"

"Hold on a minute," Scott said, sounding confused. "Lydia's mom brought Grandma Grace cookies? That was nice of her, right?"

"With an *anti-fur pamphlet* underneath!" I yelled into the phone.

"Oh, sorry, honey. I'm having a hard time hearing you. It's noisy in here."

I held my breath, imagining the words in my head I wanted to hear: *I'm worried about you, Sunflower, living with a grandmother who makes her money from animal cruelty. I'm miserable here in New Jersey, so far away from you, wondering every minute if you're going to be okay. As a matter of fact, I'm going to catch the next plane down and take you and your sister away from that horrible woman. And while I'm at it, I really miss your mom, too. Think I can convince her to come back so we can all be a family again? There're plenty of MFA programs in New Jersey, you know.*

This is what I heard instead.

"Hmmm . . . well, this sounds complicated. Can we talk about it on Friday? People keep coming in and out of the door and it's hard to have a conversation."

I twisted a strand of hair around my finger. "Okay."

"All right. We'll talk Friday. I better get back to my friends—"

"Okay, sure."

"Love you," Scott said, but I hung up the phone without saying it back. I raced upstairs and flopped down on the bed, shutting my eyes tight. I pictured Scott at a noisy restaurant, having a grand old time with his new friends, forgetting about me as soon as he hung up.

As much as I loved hearing his voice, it was the first time I wished I'd never picked up the phone to call him.

CHAPTER EIGHT

"Are we going horseback riding today?" I asked Mom on Saturday morning.

She shook her head as she put the bagels and cream cheese on the table. "Sorry, honey, I told Lindsay I'd meet her this morning to talk about the teaching position at her school. She's hoping I can take over the creative writing classes starting Monday."

Autumn groaned. "But you promised!"

"More than once," I chimed in. "You always say we're going to Ridge Gap Trail, and then when the weekend comes around you're too busy."

"I'll make it up to you," Mom said, running a hand over Autumn's hair, then giving my shoulder a squeeze. "I didn't expect things to be this busy, but I can't turn down this opportunity. We'll go out to dinner and we can rent a movie tonight, if you'd like."

"Portofino's Pizza?" Autumn asked, looking up from her bagel.

"Your choice," Mom said, and Autumn cheered. I didn't. I was tired of Mom going back on her promises, and things were probably about to get even worse if she was taking on a part-time job on top of the writing program.

"Oh, and I need a favor," Mom said. "Grandma Grace just called and said she left her inventory log at home. Can you girls ride your bikes over to her store?"

"Sure," Autumn said quickly. "Grandma told us the next time we come, we can pick out whatever we want."

I crossed my arms in front of my chest. "I'm not going."

Mom glanced over at me. "It's up to you if you want to take your grandmother up on her offer. But Autumn can't ride over there by herself."

"Fine. I'm not going in, though."

"Because she sells fur coats?" Autumn asked.

"I don't believe in cruelty to animals, and you shouldn't either. You won't believe what they do to animals to get their fur."

Mom put up a hand to stop me before I could go any further. "Okay, okay. Enough, Sunny. You don't need to frighten your sister—"

"It's not like I'm picking out a fur coat, anyway," Autumn said. "She's got lots of other stuff in her store."

"Fur coats are a very small section," Mom said to me. "And no one's forcing you to step inside. Just do me this favor, okay? Try to get along with your grandmother. She really wants to get to know you girls, and she's been more than generous to let us stay with her. Now is not the time to confront her about animal rights issues."

"But, but I thought you said you didn't like—"

"Your grandmother and I disagree on a lot of issues. But I'm working hard to make things better between us, and I hope that you'll make an effort, too."

I let out a big sigh and rolled my eyes, which Mom ignored. I couldn't believe it. She'd always said that people had to speak out against the injustices in the world, that if you sat by silently you weren't doing anything to make the world a better place.

When she was talking about speaking up to help others, I guess she wasn't including speaking up to relatives, especially a rich one who was letting us stay in her big beautiful home.

***

An hour later, we rode into the parking lot of the strip mall where Grandma Grace's store was located. "What's going on over there?" Autumn asked. "Ooo, look, a bunny!"

I glanced at the sidewalk in front of Earthly Goods where someone dressed up in a bunny suit stood waving at us. Green and blue balloons hung from the awning. "Guess it's a Grand Opening," I said as we pedaled past, parking our bikes in front of Luxury Furs and Leathers.

Autumn jumped off her bike and ran into the store. I hesitated a minute, then followed behind her, dragging my feet. If I waited outside, Grandma Grace was sure to ask questions. And since Mom had warned me about giving real answers, I figured it was easier to make a quick appearance, then scoot back outside.

The smell hit me as soon as we walked through the door—leather and something else that wasn't exactly fresh. My stomach swirled.

Autumn sneezed. I coughed.

"Hi, girls!" Grandma Grace greeted us with a big smile. "What's the matter with you two? Allergic to my shop?"

I glanced around the store, my eyes darting away from the display of fur coats in the front with the sign NEW ARRIVALS.

"Something smells funny," Autumn whispered.

"Dead animals," I whispered back.

Autumn's eyes opened wide like she'd never thought about it that way.

"Here you are," I said, handing my grandmother her notebook. "We need to get going—"

"Oh, look!" Autumn walked over to a rack of small multicolored purses. "Are these new, Grandma?"

"Just got them in yesterday. I'll tell you what. Pick out your favorite and I'll buy one for each of you as a back-to-school present."

"Really? I want the pink one," Autumn said, picking up a pink suede purse with flowers around the edges. "Come on, Sunny! How about this one?" She held up a purple purse with fringe.

I shook my head. Smelling all that leather made my mind reel. I knew how animals were turned into fur coats, but how were they changed into leather jackets and purses? I glanced down at the shoes on my feet. Or even my leather sneakers?

"No, thanks. I don't need anything," I managed to say. I didn't like the way my mind was racing, making the connection between animals and clothing and even the food I ate.

"Go ahead," Grandma Grace said. "They're soft as velvet."

I shook my head again. Soft as velvet made me think of Stellaluna's fur, which made me think of the fur coats on the racks. I bit my lip to keep from yelling, "You're not selling luxury items! You're selling cruelty and death!"

My cheeks were heating up, and I knew I had to get out of that place quick. "Um, I'm going to pick up something at the bookstore. I'll be back in a few minutes," I said and bolted out the door.

***

"Look what I got!" Autumn showed off the pink purse that hung from her shoulder as she walked out of the shop a few minutes later. "See, no fur on it!"

I shrugged and looked away from my sister. "Hey, you want to check out Earthly Goods?" I was a little curious about Lydia's store, and I wondered how she'd act when she saw me.

"Sure," Autumn said. "Did you get anything at the bookstore?"

I shook my head no as we hopped on our bikes and pedaled down the sidewalk to Earthly Goods. The person in the bunny costume handed us a twenty percent off coupon and we stepped inside.

I breathed in strong incense as I looked around. Candles and soap sat on tables with colorful tablecloths, Be Kind to Animals and Save the Earth posters lined the walls, and the shelves were stocked with everything from shampoo to vegan donuts.

"Wow!" Autumn said as we walked up and down the aisles. "This place is cool. Hey, there's free samples!"

Lydia stood in front of a small table. She didn't smile when she saw me, but she held out her tray. "Tofutti? There's chocolate chip mint and chocolate peanut butter."

"What's Tofutti?" I asked.

"Ice cream made from tofu."

I wrinkled my nose.

"Try some," Lydia said.

A short lady with lots of long, curly hair the same color as Lydia's came out from behind the counter. "Do you girls know each other?"

"We have language arts together," I said.

"I'm Darlene Applebaum." She held out her hand to shake mine the same way Lydia had on the first day of school. "It's great to meet a new friend of Lydia's!"

"We're not friends, Mom. We just have a class together," Lydia said.

"Well, that's a start," Mrs. Applebaum said.

I avoided Lydia's eyes, sticking the spoonful of Tofutti in my mouth. It wasn't bad. I turned to my sister. "You should try some, Autumn."

Mrs. Applebaum handed Autumn a cup. "Chocolate peanut butter's my favorite."

"Mmm, yum," Autumn said. "What's tofu made out of?"

"Soybeans," Lydia answered.

Autumn made a face.

"Actually," Lydia said, her expression softening, "You can do anything with tofu. You can make the yummiest cheesecake or peanut butter pie. You just blend up the silken tofu to make it nice and creamy and then you put all your regular

ingredients in. Or you can make tofu hot dogs. We had a
neighbor try ours and she said it tasted just like a regular hot
dog! Not that I would know, since I've never eaten meat in my
whole entire life. There're also tofu burgers, barbecued tofu,
fried tofu . . ."

Autumn's eyes got really big and Lydia grinned. I found
myself grinning, too.

"It really is the miracle food," Mrs. Applebaum said.

"We'll have to get Mom to come back and buy some," I
told my sister.

We wandered around the store a little more, stopping at
another free sample table with chips and dips. While Autumn
nibbled, I headed over to a table full of pamphlets that sat in
the back corner. After a quick glance, I knew they were all
about cruelty to animals. I picked up a handful and slipped
them into the bag with my magazine. Then I noticed a sign
on the bulletin board:

**Animal Rights Group Forming Now! Join
us for our first meeting on October 12 to dis-
cuss our protest for Fur-Free Friday!**

**Contact Darlene Applebaum for more
details: 555-381-0150**

"Sunny?" Autumn called. I quickly turned away from the table and ran to meet her.

"I'm definitely asking Mom to come back here." Autumn held up another cup of Tofutti. "Chocolate peanut butter is the best."

"Yeah," I said. "What do you think Grandma Grace will say if she hears we got something at Earthly Goods?"

Autumn giggled as we headed out the door. "I guess we won't tell her, will we?"

***

When we got home, I went straight to my room, shutting the door behind me. A new idea was brewing in my head, and I wanted to get to work on it right away. First, I stuck the pamphlets in my desk drawer under my notebooks, the same place I'd hidden the one Grandma Grace found under the cookies. I'd read enough animal rights literature for now. But someday, when I was feeling brave, I'd read all of them.

Next, I turned my attention to my main problem: getting Mom and Scott back together. Logging into my Chrome Book, I typed in "How to Get Noticed by Your Crush." It was a headline I saw on a *Seventeen* magazine in the bookstore, and while I didn't have enough money to buy the magazine, I figured I could find the same thing on the Internet.

Sure enough, tons of articles popped up. I clicked on the first one:

> First impressions count. Pay special attention to your appearance. Focus on being active and full of positive energy. Most importantly, always remember that when you are confident in yourself, others will be, too.

I thought about that for a minute. Mom seemed confident, all right. She believed in herself and didn't let anything stop her. In fact, that's what had gotten us into this trouble to begin with; she wanted to go back to school no matter what anyone else thought about it. I didn't see how that made her more attractive to Scott, but I just shrugged and read on.

> Step 1: Take a little extra time when you're getting ready in the morning. You don't want to look like you've rolled straight out of bed.

Hmm . . . Mom was always in a rush and didn't seem to spend much time worrying about her appearance at all. Maybe we were on to something here.

I continued to read, paying special attention to the beauty advice: "Be bold when you apply your makeup, and touch up when you need to," "Try a new style for an extra confidence boost," and my favorite piece of advice, "Wear red."

According to the article, it seemed my mom was a perfect candidate for a makeover. It would make Mom feel better about herself, and that would make Scott notice her again, even if she didn't realize he was supposed to be her "crush." The only problem? Mom seemed perfectly happy the way she was.

The article didn't say anything about an unwilling subject. But as I read it over again, I knew it was worth a try. After Mom's makeover, I'd send her new and improved photo to Scott. He'd take one look at the picture, and it would knock him right over. He'd walk around all day in a starry-eyed haze (according to the article). Those lost feelings would come rushing back, and he'd remember how he and Mom were once deeply in love.

Scott would start acting more romantic, sending flowers and cute cards and giving Mom lots of compliments, the way boyfriends were supposed to. Mom would remember how great things used to be, and she'd give up dinners with her new "friends."

Once they both realized they belonged together, Mom would find a school in New Jersey, and we'd move back home and live happily ever after.

End of story. Now all I had to do was convince Mom it was time for a makeover.

SUNNY'S SUPER-STUPENDOUS PLAN TO GET MOM AND DAD BACK TOGETHER

13. Convince Mom she needs a makeover. Buy her a red shirt because "studies show that a person looks more attractive to someone else when he/she wears red." Snap her photo afterward, and send it to Scott in a sparkly frame with hearts around the border.

CHAPTER NINE

"I won't be home for dinner tonight," Mom said Monday morning. "Grandma Grace is making her special macaroni and cheese."

"Really?" Autumn jumped up and down in her seat so that her pigtails bounced. "Mac and cheese is my favorite!"

"Sunny's, too," Mom said, smiling at me.

Macaroni and cheese was beside the point. And just because Grandma Grace was making my favorite meal, it didn't mean I had to like her any better. "Where are you going?"

"I'm meeting with my critique partner. Our short stories are due on Friday and I still have a lot of work to do."

"What's her name?" I asked.

"Actually, his name is Jeb—"

"Jeb? What kind of a name is that?" I asked. Autumn giggled.

"A perfectly good name," Mom said, ruffling my hair. "Look, Sunny, meeting with other students is a requirement. And Grandma Grace offered to make your favorite dinner so I'm sure you'll be fine."

I shrugged away from her. "Did you tell Scott you're going to dinner with Jeb?"

"Scott doesn't have anything to do with this. But if I told him, I'm sure he wouldn't mind."

"Hmph." I gobbled down my toast and excused myself to send a quick email to Scott. As soon as I hit SEND, I got this awful feeling inside. What if Mom was right, and Scott didn't care?

***

When I got to school, Mrs. Rodriguez, the librarian, stopped me in the hall. "The list is posted," she half-said, half-sang.

I gave her a funny look. "What list?"

"The list for the OM teams. It's on the media center front window. Make sure you check it."

"Okay," I said with a shrug. Who wanted to look at a list that didn't have your name on it? I was sure I'd messed up with the last prompt. When I saw the wedding cake, I was so busy thinking about Mom and Scott that I had to scribble something down at the last minute. Something really stupid.

"And by the way, Sunny?"

I turned around. I didn't even know Mrs. Rodriguez knew my name.

"That last prompt, for the wedding cake?" She winked at me. "Very clever response."

"Thanks." My heart sped up. I thought about what I'd written. *You'd never suspect the bride and groom are really undercover FBI agents who are about to search the cake for the hidden code inside.* It seemed like a dumb response at the time, especially when everyone else was probably saying stuff like "Love is Sweet" because they were cutting a wedding cake.

Maybe this was what Coach Baker meant by "thinking outside the box"?

I hurried to the media center, waiting until a small group of kids moved away from the entrance. Then I took my finger and ran it down the list. "Lydia Applebaum, Sunny Beringer . . ."

I didn't realize I'd squealed until I'd spun around and ran smack into Lydia, who was standing behind me. "You made it!" I told her. "We both made the team."

Lydia didn't shout or jump up and down. She rocked back and forth on her toes a minute, and a smile curved up the corners of her mouth. Then she straightened it.

"Congratulations," she said, then walked past me to look at the list herself.

***

When I got home that afternoon, I knew it was time to put all that creative energy to work. I headed to the backyard gazebo with my notebook. Sitting down on the bench, I looked back over Sunny's Super-Stupendous Plan. First, I had to buy some makeup and a special red shirt for Mom's makeover. Next, I had to save up some money to buy a gift certificate to a restaurant, the kind with candlelight and violins. That would have to wait until Scott came to visit, which wouldn't be until . . . Christmas.

I chewed on my pen. Christmas was over two months away. It was a long time to wait, especially now that Mom was going on dinner dates with Jeb, and Scott was going out with "friends."

A thought popped into my head, and not for the first time either. *Maybe it was already too late.*

Maybe things had changed between Mom and Scott for good. Maybe they'd decided they didn't want us to live together as a family anymore.

And if Mom's and Scott's feelings had changed, what could I really do about it? A fancy new makeover, a romantic restaurant . . . could that influence what they felt deep down in their hearts?

I looked up from my notebook, staring out at the big stretch of green yard bordered with large trees. It was beautiful here in Bennetsville, but it wasn't my home. Home was with Mom and Scott, with all of us together. Somehow, I had to believe there was still hope. Because without hope, I didn't have a place where I belonged.

I looked back down at my notebook, doodling along the edges of the paper to fire up some new creative thoughts. And as I sketched, the image of the bride and groom gazing at each other over the wedding cake began to take shape. The photo had stuck in my mind ever since I saw it at OM tryouts, making me wonder about the relationship between my parents. Maybe if I made a photo album for Mom's birthday it would bring back some old memories.

It could remind Mom of what she was missing. All our photos were loaded on the computer so if I printed them out and put them together in a book, it would tell the story of our lives.

It would be super easy.

Mom had been too busy chasing crazy goals of MFAs. But she'd slow down and pay attention when I handed her the photo album. She had to! She'd remember how she missed Scott's smile, his laughter, and his kindness. She'd realize that she couldn't live without him, and that we couldn't live without him either.

I stood up from the bench, eager to get started on the album. I was almost at the back door when I heard it. A rustling coming from the bushes near the hammock. I glanced at the corner of the yard, catching a glimpse of caramel-colored fur beneath the leaves.

A cat! My heart sped up right away as I thought of Stellaluna. I turned and tiptoed closer. Kneeling down in the grass, I held out my hand and waited. The cat kept her distance, staring out at me with unblinking yellow eyes.

"Who are you?" I whispered, noticing that she wasn't wearing a collar. "Do you belong to anyone?"

Her tail swished back and forth, but she didn't come any closer.

The door slammed, and the cat took off under the bushes. "Sunny!" Autumn called. "What are you looking at?"

"Nothing." I got to my feet quickly and headed back to the house. I wasn't willing to tell Autumn about the cat. The last thing I needed was for her to blab about it to Grandma Grace, who would probably call the pound. Someone who sold the fur coats off animals' backs would never allow me to feed a stray cat in her yard.

I followed my sister back inside the house, pretending to be interested while she told me all about how Danny Peters got in trouble for letting the class salamander out of its cage. I couldn't do anything for Stellaluna right now, but I could keep this new cat safe.

After I talked to Autumn, I headed straight to the computer. Scrolling through files, I noticed they were all marked with dates, so I went back to the earliest ones: millions of photos of me when I was a baby. Swinging, laughing, crying, in the bathtub, even sitting in my high chair with smushed peas all over my face. Why Mom thought that was something she needed to take a picture of, I'll never understand. I guess it was the same reason she had pictures of me crawling around on the floor totally naked.

Autumn came up behind me and laughed when she saw a picture of my naked bottom.

"Don't worry," I told her. "I'm sure she has plenty of you without any clothes on, too."

Autumn snorted. "Why are you looking at baby pictures? School project?"

I shook my head. "Just doing a little research." I didn't want to tell her about the photo album I was making for Mom. Autumn couldn't keep a secret for a minute. "I mean, yeah, it's something for school."

"Oh." Autumn stood by my shoulder and watched as I scrolled through more pictures. I was glad when she got bored and walked away a few minutes later.

This was going to take a while. Each file had tons of baby pictures, and most of them looked nearly the same. I looked for the ones that had both Mom and Scott in them, but I couldn't find any. In most of the pictures I was by myself. A photo album of me doing baby tricks wasn't exactly going to accomplish my goal. I went back a few more months to December.

Bingo! Mom and Scott in the hospital right after I was born. I sure was an ugly little thing. My face was all red and squinched up and my eyes were closed. My face looked like a newborn guinea pig's before the fur grows in.

But Mom and Scott were gazing down at me like I was the most beautiful thing they'd ever seen. Anyone could see the connection running between the two of them as Mom held me and Scott leaned over with his arm around her. This photo spelled out "family."

"Hey." Mom touched my shoulder and I jumped about a hundred feet. She laughed. "Sorry, didn't mean to scare you. What're you up to?"

I settled back down on the seat. "Oh, just looking at some old photos. Can you believe how different Scott looks here?"

Mom sucked in her breath as she leaned in to take a closer look. Her hair was longer in the photo and didn't have gray streaks like it did now. Besides that, she looked exactly the same. Scott's hair was longer, too, falling over his forehead and all the way to his shoulders. It curled at the bottom, even though now it was perfectly straight. Plus, he wasn't wearing glasses even though he always said he was blind as a bat without them.

The picture seemed to take Mom by surprise. She hadn't said a word. "Mom?" I finally asked.

She exhaled, long and slow.

"Mom?" I said again. When she didn't answer I turned to look at her.

Her eyes had filled with tears.

"Are you okay?"

"Um, yeah." She swallowed and shook her head. "Honey, about the photo . . ."

"I love it. But how come there aren't any other pictures of the three of us right after I was born?"

Mom took another deep breath. "There's something I need to tell you."

I looked over at her. "What? Is it about my birth mom?"

Another long pause.

"What, Mom? What do you need to tell me?"

The look on Mom's face flickered and disappeared. It was like watching a slide show, and we'd moved to a slide that showed something totally different. Mom cleared her throat and spoke slowly, choosing her words very carefully. "Oh, um, nothing. Just that your birth mother invited us into the delivery room, so we could watch you being born."

"Eww," I said. "Gross!"

"It wasn't gross." Mom put an arm around me. "It was amazing. The miracle of life."

"I would have told her to call me *after* the baby showed up," I said.

Mom laughed. But it was a hollow sound. "Okay. Let me know when you finish your trip down memory lane," she said, sounding like herself again. In control. "I have some files I need to transfer to my laptop."

"All right." I marked the photo number in my notebook. Mom was trying to cover, but I knew something was up. I hadn't imagined her reaction. And if there was a picture with Mom, Scott, and me in our files, there had to be more. Mom might be able to walk away from one photo, but a whole album? That wouldn't be so easy to ignore.

SUNNY'S SUPER-STUPENDOUS PLAN TO GET MOM AND DAD BACK TOGETHER

14. Make a photo album with lots of pictures of Mom and Scott when they were young and in love. Include a few pictures of Autumn and me to show how we glued them together as one big happy family. Give it to Mom on her birthday.

CHAPTER TEN

From: SunnyKid@CreativityisCool.com
To: MadelineL@ilovebooks.com
Good News!

I can't believe it! I made the OM team! It's really a big deal here. There are two teams and last year they both went to Worlds. I'm glad I made it, but I'd much rather be on the team with you at Alexander!

From: MadelineL@ilovebooks.com
To: SunnyKid@CreativityisCool.com
Re: Good News!

Congrats on making the OM team! We're having our first meeting next week. Emma Galindo said she's coming with me to see what it's all about!

***

"Before we get started," Coach Baker said at our first official OM meeting, "we're going to do a little activity to get to know one another better. A few of you know one another from last year, but some of you may feel like you've landed in a group of complete strangers. Don't worry, in a few weeks, all of you will feel like a team. You have the Baker-Nelson guarantee."

A few kids laughed. Not me. I glanced up and down the table. I was glad to see that Dragon Boy, whose name was actually Avi Sterling, had made the team, too. Not that he said a word to me. And Lydia was definitely not turning cartwheels about getting to work with me either.

"What I'd like for you to do is write a short rhyming poem that includes your name and shares something important about yourself. Everybody got it?"

"Sure thing!"

"Got it!"

A few people nodded, and then a girl who'd been on the team last year asked, "How much time do we have?"

"Four minutes," Coach Baker said. "And . . . go!"

Everyone scrambled for notebooks and pencils. I love to write, but not under pressure. And I certainly didn't want to read my poem aloud. To strangers. Even Baker had said that's who they were. But I racked my brain and this is what I came up with:

My name's Sunny
And I like to drink tea,
But mostly I love to draw things that I see
That's because drawing makes me feel free.
So if I had to put it to the test
Art's the thing that I like best.

As soon as Coach Baker read my poem aloud I realized I should have left out the part about tea. Plus, it sounded like something a second grader would write. But I didn't feel as embarrassed when I heard some of the others. Even Lydia, with all her creative writing classes, hadn't written anything much better than mine:

My name's Lydia A.
I love animals today
And tomorrow, too.
And so should you!
I never eat meat.
It's not a treat
If you're the one dead
Instead of the one being fed.

"I know it's not that great," Lydia said with a shrug after he read her poem, "but, Coach Baker, what did you expect? You only gave us four minutes!"

"Exactly." Baker grinned. "When we get into the Spontaneous round of the competition, you'll have to learn to think on your feet. Odyssey of the Mind is all about making choices, and putting those choices into action."

The words echoed in my head. *Choices. Action.*

"All right," Coach Baker said when everyone had finished sharing their poems. "Good job, guys. Now it's time to choose a long-term team problem. Read over all five choices and study them carefully. Then we'll have a respectful discussion." He paused and looked at all of us. "Note that I said *respectful discussion*, not argument."

The room went quiet as Coach Baker passed out name tags and sheets of paper with the different problems and descriptions. I looked down at my paper. The five categories were familiar to me: we had to choose between building a vehicle, putting on a skit that had a lot of technical details involving scientific samples, putting on a musical theater production based on the classics, building something out of balsa wood, or performing a humorous skit.

I knew nothing about building a vehicle, so I immediately crossed out Problem 1: "Ooh-motional Vehicle." I wasn't big on technical stuff like special effects, so I crossed out Problem 2: "Weird Science" and Problem 4: "You Make the Call," the balsa wood problem. That left Problems 3 and 5.

I read the first line of the description for Problem 3: "Teams will put a musical theater spin on one of William Shakespeare's famous lines, 'To be or not to be.'"

Shakespeare? My hand flew to my forehead. The only thing I knew about Shakespeare was this quote Mom kept on the bulletin board in her office: "To thine own self be true." When I asked Mom what it meant, she said it was about being the person you were supposed to be deep inside, and not worrying so much about what other people thought of you.

All I knew was that Shakespeare spoke in riddles, and I wasn't crazy about singing in front of everyone either. I skipped to Problem 5: "Odyssey Angels." It looked like a lot of fun. Nothing too technical, no required song-and-dance . . . just a humorous skit about angels.

I crossed my fingers under the table, hoping my new team members would feel the same way I did.

Coach Baker started the discussion a few minutes later.

"I think we should build the vehicle," said a boy whose name tag read Carson Fullers. He must have been an eighth grader because he was twice my height and about twice as wide. "I know how to rig up a brake suspension system."

A couple of kids echoed him, commenting how cool building a vehicle would be. Someone said something about figuring out how to propel it with power steering. One boy reached for his notebook and began sketching.

My stomach twisted and I crossed the fingers of my other hand, as well.

"I think we should do a musical theater skit about Shakespeare," Lydia said. "We did Shakespeare monologues at our homeschool co-op last year and it was a lot of fun!"

"I'm with Lydia," said Jalia. "My mom teaches Shakespeare in her classes at the university, and I've seen some of the plays. We could come up with a million puns and all kinds of word-play if we were doing Shakespeare."

I looked over at Jalia, recognizing her from math class. She had light brown skin and curly dark hair, and wore small round glasses. I wasn't surprised by Lydia's choice, but who would have guessed there was another sixth grader who actually loved Shakespeare, too? I clenched my fingers tighter.

Avi spoke up for the first time. "I'm for Weird Science. We'd get to travel to outer space."

"How about you, Sunny?" Coach Baker asked. "Which problem are you most interested in?"

"Um, how about Problem Five?" I uncrossed my cramped fingers and ran my hands up and down my jeans to loosen them up. Staying quiet was obviously not getting me any-where. "I'm not good at technical stuff, and I don't know a thing about Shakespeare except it's really hard to understand. So I think we should pick Odyssey Angels."

Someone groaned, and Coach Baker said, "We need to listen to everyone's opinion here. We're a team now, remember?"

"You don't have to know Shakespeare to choose Problem Three," Lydia said. "It's all about making the wrong choices."

I shrugged. "We'd have to build a trapdoor," I said, pointing to that part of the description. "*And* I'm a terrible singer."

"You won't have to do a solo," Jalia said. "We'll sing together."

"Forget the singing," Carson said. "Let's build a vehicle!"

The discussion went on and on for a long time until it sounded more like an argument. Finally, Coach Baker blew his whistle. "Your homework is to write down three good reasons for choosing a particular problem. Everyone will make his or her case next week, and then we'll vote."

I packed up my stuff and followed Lydia outside to wait for my mom. I stood there quietly until Lydia said, "So if it's a choice between the vehicle and Shakespeare, which one will you vote for?"

"I don't want to do the vehicle—"

"That's what I thought." A triumphant smile flashed across her face. "If you don't want to get stuck with the vehicle, just make sure you vote for Shakespeare next week. We'll outnumber them for sure."

"There are seven of us on the team," I pointed out. "And even if I vote with you and Jalia, that only makes three."

"Avi's the wild card," Lydia said. "But don't worry, Jalia and I will take care of him. He'll vote on our side. I'm sure of it."

I crossed my arms in front of my chest. "I already told you, Lydia, I don't want to do the Shakespeare skit. And what makes you so sure Avi won't vote for the vehicle?"

"He won't, any more than you will," Lydia said.

"You don't know everything," I said, getting more annoyed with her by the second. I took a slow deep breath to stay calm. "Maybe I'll convince Avi and one of the other boys to go with Odyssey Angels instead."

"Now that," Lydia said, giving me a know-it-all grin, "is unlikely." She slung her backpack over her shoulder as a small blue car covered with bumper stickers pulled up to the curb. One of the stickers jumped out from the others: CRUEL PEOPLE WEAR FUR.

Lydia's mom rolled down the window. "Hi, Sunny! How's it going?"

"Great," I managed to say through gritted teeth. As the car pulled away, I tried not to think about the bumper sticker. Even though Lydia got on my nerves, we were on the same side about animal rights. I wished I could tell her how I felt about furs, but that would mean telling her my grandmother owned Luxury Furs and Leathers. She'd expect me to do whatever it took to get my grandmother to shut down her store. Lydia would never understand that I was stuck right in the middle.

That meant it was up to me to make sure she never found out who really owned the fur store right down the sidewalk from Earthly Goods.

CHAPTER ELEVEN

From: MadelineL@ilovebooks.com
To: SunnyKid@CreativityisCool.com
Ooh-Motional Vehicle!

We picked our OM problem! We're doing Ooh-Motional Vehicle! It's going to be so cool. Trent says he knows how to build a car because he did the soapbox derby.

Wish you were here!

From: SunnyKid@CreativityisCool.com
To: MadelineL@ilovebooks.com
Re: Ooh-Motional Vehicle!

We still haven't decided on our problem. There was a big argument about it. I don't know anything about making cars and I don't want to do musical theater because, as you know, *I can't sing*!

There's one girl who is going to be really angry if I don't pick musical theater, but I'm not sure what I'm going to vote for next week.

Do you think I should vote for the car, Weird Science, or my favorite that no one else likes. . . . Odyssey Angels???

From: MadelineL@ilovebooks.com
To: SunnyKid@CreativityisCool.com
Re: Ooh-Motional Vehicle!

Of course you can sing! Just stay away from the high notes. Who knows? Maybe if you vote for the angels, others will join you.

Don't worry about making someone mad. She'll get over it! ☺

P.S. Did I tell you Emma G. is on my team this year?

***

I stared at Madeline's email for a long time before I hit DELETE. I'd been so excited to see her name pop up on the computer screen, but now I wished I had never read it. I'd never been crazy about Emma G. I wondered if she was trying to replace me as Madeline's best friend when, here I was, stuck in North Carolina where I didn't have any friends at all.

Madeline's email was still on my mind as I sat in my usual spot at lunch the following Wednesday pretending like I was paying attention to the conversation, which was sprinkled with a lot of boys' names and a lot of talk about what someone had heard somebody say about somebody else. That's when Lydia walked right up to our table.

"Did you change your mind about the problem?" she asked me. She'd dropped the overly confident tone I'd heard after last week's meeting, and I could hear a hint of worry in her voice. "Please, please, tell me you're voting for Problem Three."

"I guess you'll have to wait for the meeting," I said.

"Well, can I see what you wrote? I'll show you mine," Lydia said, handing me a folded piece of paper.

"That's okay," I said, shaking my head. I noticed the table had gone completely quiet, and I was ready for her to take her persuasive paper and go back to wherever she usually sat in the cafeteria.

"Um, well, okay." Lydia looked unsure of herself for the first time as she put the folded piece of paper back in her pocket. "It's just that I really don't want to do Ooh-motional Vehicle. I'll go with Weird Science before I vote for that."

"What are ya'll talking about?" Jessie asked, wrinkling up her nose. "Weird Science? Ooh-motional Vehicle?"

"It's for Odyssey of the Mind," I told her. "Lydia and I are on the same team."

"Yeah, I heard about that on the announcements," Cassie said. "It must be a team of weirdos, because Avi Sterling's in it, too."

"Who's Avi Sterling?" Chloe asked.

"He's this short kid with glasses whose hair sticks out all over his head, like Einstein," Cassie said.

"Oh, yeah, I've seen him in the hall!" Meghan said with a giggle.

Cassie rolled her eyes. "He is a complete nerd!"

My stomach flipped. *Say something*, I told myself. *Tell them Avi's a nice kid, and they shouldn't make fun of someone because of the way he looks!*

But my mouth stayed shut, like I'd swallowed a big spoonful of peanut butter.

"Avi Sterling is super smart," Lydia said. "Who cares if his hair sticks up?"

Cassie snorted.

"So what's Odyssey of the Mind all about anyway?" Jessie asked me.

"We have to write a skit," I told her. "And then we compete against other OM teams."

"It's much more than that," Lydia interrupted. "It's all about creativity. And using your brain."

"Wow, sounds like fun," Cassie said, making it sound as much fun as ten pages of math homework.

"It *is* loads of fun," Lydia protested, turning to Cassie. "Don't knock something until you've tried it."

"'Don't knock something until you've tried it,'" Cassie mimicked, and some of the girls giggled.

My cheeks got hot. I knew I should speak up, but I still couldn't get myself to.

Lydia hesitated, and when I didn't say anything else to her either, she said, "Well, I guess I'll see you after school, Sunny. No hard feelings, okay?"

"Yeah, sure," I managed as Lydia walked away from the table.

"What a loser," Cassie said under her breath.

Words got stuck in my throat again. What was wrong with me? In New Jersey, I was nice to everyone. I'd never hurt someone's feelings on purpose.

"Hey, Sunny," Jessie said. "I've got the greatest idea! You should come to the Drama Club meeting with me after school today. They'll need someone who's good at art to work on scenery."

"You're joining Drama Club?" Chloe asked. "I thought you were trying out for the cheerleading squad."

"I am," Jessie said. "Who says I can't do both?"

Chloe shrugged. "I didn't know you were going out for Drama Club, that's all. You never mentioned it."

"Yeah," Cassie added. "There're a lot of weird kids in Drama Club."

"So what? It sounds like fun." Jessie turned to me. "What do you think, Sunny? Will you meet me after school?"

I shook my head. "I can't. Odyssey of the Mind meets every Wednesday."

"Well," Jessie said, "OM sounds interesting, and all, but we'll fill up the auditorium for the plays. I could get a starring role, and kids will think it's cool if we're in the club together." Jessie turned to the rest of the table. "Come on, ya'll. We should all go to the meeting today. It'll be fun!"

"No, thanks," Cassie said, and the other girls shook their heads and started offering up excuses. While Jessie was trying to make her case, I got the idea that Cassie was the one who decided what was cool and what wasn't. Maybe she stunk at singing and acting, so it was easier to make fun of something when she knew she could never get a starring role.

Jessie turned back to me. "You can do Odyssey of the Mind *and* Drama Club. Today's the first meeting, so we'll talk about what the best day is for everyone. I'm sure we can convince them to not choose Wednesday. Come on. You'll love it."

I tucked my hair behind my ears and took a sip from my juice box. Jessie didn't have any idea about what I loved—she hardly even knew me. But then she grabbed my wrist and gave me one of her sparkly grins, in a totally BFF way. "Come on, Sunny, say you'll come with me today . . ."

I sputtered and the juice squirted back out, through my nose. Jessie dropped my wrist, and I wiped at my face with the back of my hand. "I, uh, I just remembered. I have a doctor's appointment after school, so I can't go with you."

Jessie crossed her arms in front of her chest. "You *just* remembered?"

"Yeah. My mom will be waiting for me."

"Whatever."

She was annoyed, but I couldn't tell if she believed me about the appointment. *I just lied to Jessie*, I thought, as the conversation returned to its usual ping-pong of names. *If Jessie finds out I lied, she'll probably dump me. Just like I did to Lydia that day she brought eggplant for lunch.*

I'd competed for a spot on the OM team and earned it. I loved OM. But was it worth giving up the chance to be part of the popular crowd? I thought about it for the rest of lunch.

By the time the bell rang, I still didn't have an answer.

CHAPTER TWELVE

When the last bell rang, I followed the crowd out the front doors. I stood under the covered walkway trying to look like I was waiting for my mom, but I was just wasting time while I decided what to do. Jessie really wanted me to go to the drama club meeting, and if I didn't go, I might lose my invitation to sit at her lunch table, and then where would I be? I'd dumped Avi after a week and treated Lydia even worse. Besides, I'd noticed they both had found other kids to sit with.

Missing one meeting didn't mean I had to quit the OM team for good.

Except. Except that today was the day of the big vote, and if I didn't show up and share my thoughts, Coach Baker might choose someone else for the team. Of course, quitting OM would solve the problem about what to vote for, and it meant I wouldn't have to deal with Lydia anymore either. But I wasn't a quitter. Not only that, I loved Odyssey of the Mind. I'd earned my spot and giving it up would be like giving up on myself. Or, at least the person I'd always been.

As the building cleared out, I felt my feet begin to move forward. Before I realized what was happening, I'd taken off at a run toward the media center, grabbing my seat right as the meeting got started.

"Okay, settle down, everyone." Coach Baker held up his hand to get our attention. "I'm assuming everyone has put some thought into their choices for the Long-Term Problem. Now it's time to use your arguments to convince your team members. Who'd like to go first?"

Coach Baker called on Lydia since she was waving her hand wildly in the air. I sat on top of my hands, hoping everyone else would be as eager to share their thoughts as Lydia. I'd given up on the idea of Odyssey Angels since no one else had been interested in it. Instead of writing up my reasons for my choice, I was hoping that by the time Coach Baker called on me, it would be easier to cast a deciding vote. If someone had defected from the vehicle side and had chosen Weird Science instead, I could cast the winning vote, so it would be 3–2–2 in favor of Weird Science.

Unfortunately, after five members had read their long and detailed speeches, it was 3–2 in favor of the Ooh-motional Vehicle. It was down to Avi and me.

"All right, who wants to go next?" Coach Baker asked, looking at both of us. I bit my lip. It looked like no matter what I chose, I'd be stuck doing a problem I wasn't interested in.

I glanced over at Lydia, who gave me a pleading look. Somehow, looking across the table at her, I got that funny feeling in my stomach again, the one I'd had after I'd walked away from her in the cafeteria. Even though I'd tried to apologize, it didn't change what I had done. I hadn't defended her when the other girls made rude comments and I'd chosen them over her. She'd been awfully bossy in telling me which problem to pick, but I owed her one.

"I think we should do 'To Be or Not to Be,'" I said, still looking at Lydia. A smile spread across her face, and I felt one tugging at the corners of my mouth, too. "It's about making bad choices and learning from them. Plus, I don't know anything about building a vehicle."

Jalia and Lydia cheered, and that's when Avi said, "I think musical theater will be fun. I helped with the choreography for a play at church, and I'm pretty good at writing songs."

I stared at Avi, surprised. Not only was it the most I'd ever heard him say, but I'd never expected him to have musical theater talents. Lydia and Jalia hugged each other while the vehicle crew mumbled about how disappointed they were.

"Looks like we have a decision!" Coach Baker boomed out. "Problem number three it is!"

Lydia gave Jalia a high five, but when I tried to join in the celebration, she opened her notebook and started scribbling. The smile she'd given me a few minutes earlier was wiped clean from her face.

***

After school, I was still thinking about Lydia as I slipped a saucer of tuna under the bushes in the backyard. As much as Lydia annoyed me, I was glad we were on the same OM team. There was something about her that seemed genuine, same as with Avi, the boy I'd thought of only as "Dragon Boy" for weeks. Again, I wondered if Lydia and I might actually be friends if I could just get up the courage to tell her I felt the same way she did about the fur store.

I heard leaves rustle and turned to see the caramel-colored cat making her way across the yard. I'd only seen the cat twice in the last couple of weeks, but I knew she'd been coming around because the plates were always empty when I checked.

She moved boldly, as if she were no longer afraid of me. Maybe she knew I was the one who'd been leaving food for her.

I crouched down and stretched out my hand. "Come here, kitty," I called softly.

And then I waited. And waited. She finally made her way over, pushing her head up against my hand. "You came back," I said. "You don't have a home, do you?"

She rubbed against my legs, her tail swishing back and forth, and it filled me up with happiness inside. For now, I couldn't help the animals used to make the fur coats in Grandma Grace's store, but I could help a little stray cat by feeding her every day.

"I'll name you Ripple," I told her. It was the title of one of Scott's favorite songs. He loved to play it on the guitar. Besides, it was the perfect name for a cat with fur like fudge ripple ice cream.

The cat mewed. "You like that, huh? Ripple it is."

She stayed with me for a while, until a noise in the distance scared her back into the bushes.

After sticking the saucer in the dishwasher, I headed to the office to go through the last of the files. When I got to the photos taken right before we left New Jersey, I counted up the numbers I'd written in my notebook. Ten. Only ten photos of just Mom and Scott together, from the day I was born until now. I'd found plenty of all of us together, but the album I was making was supposed to show how much they were in love with each other, not with their kids.

I needed photos of the two of them when they first started dating. Unfortunately, the earliest files on the computer started with my birthday.

I sighed and got up to find my mom. She was standing in front of the stove cooking dinner. "Mom, what did you do with the photos of you and Scott when you first met?"

She looked up at me. "You mean back when we were in college?"

"Yeah." I grinned. "From the olden days, back when you were young."

"I suppose they're around here somewhere."

"Where do you think they are?"

Mom frowned, then turned back to the pasta sauce she was stirring. "I'm not exactly sure. We packed up boxes of stuff and put them in storage before we left."

I groaned.

"What's wrong? Do you need the old photos for a school project?"

I paused, scooping up some parmesan cheese from the cutting board and dropping it in my mouth. "Um, yeah," I said after I swallowed. "A school project."

"Well, if you really need the pictures, you could ask Scott. I bet he has a few boxes of old photos lying around somewhere."

"Okay." At least it wasn't a total dead end. "How did you two meet, anyway?"

"Oh, freshman year, I guess."

"In what class? Or did you meet on campus?"

Mom stared down at the sauce. Then she started sprinkling in spices, a teaspoon of this, a teaspoon of that. Finally, she dropped the spoon against the side of the pot and wiped her hands on her jeans. "In class. I think it was English or psychology or something. It was a long time ago, Sunny."

"I know that." I sat down at the kitchen table, tucking my feet underneath me on the chair. Mom didn't have a bit of romance in her. She couldn't even remember where they first met! "Where did you go on your first date?"

Mom started stirring the sauce again. Round and round the spoon went, like she was trying to figure out the answer to one of the world's greatest mysteries.

"Mom?" I asked again.

"Oh, sorry," she said, screwing the caps on the jars of spices and putting them back in the rack.

"I asked you where you went on your first date with Scott."

"First date? Hate to disappoint you, but I really can't remember."

"Oh." I twisted a strand of my hair. "Well, what did you used to do together for fun?"

"We were mostly friends at first. There was a group of us that hung out together. Though we haven't really stayed in touch with most of them. I wonder what Miranda and Kenny are doing these days. We were both in their wedding, you know."

"Why didn't you and Scott get married after college?" I asked, even though I'd asked the question many times before. Maybe this time, I'd get a different answer. "You were dating as long as Miranda and Kenny were."

Mom paused. Another long one. This time I was going to wait her out.

"Oh, I don't know. . . . Neither of us was interested in marriage, I guess. What's with all the questions tonight, anyway? I'm sure you don't need this kind of information for a school project."

"Just curious. You never talk about it."

Mom shrugged and stared into the pot like she'd find her memories there.

"It seems like if someone has been dating for years and years that they'd want to get married—"

"That's not how it was with us," Mom said, but her voice had changed. It had a finality to it. She was finished with the conversation. She glanced up at the clock. "Do you mind watching the sauce for a while? It needs to simmer for about twenty minutes. Stir it once in a while, okay? I need to finish my critique before the chat room tonight."

"Oh, okay." Before I could say another word, Mom had walked out of the room, leaving me with the simmering pasta sauce and a whole lot of unanswered questions.

CHAPTER THIRTEEN

Jessie didn't look up at me when I walked into art class the next day. She didn't look up when my chair scraped against the concrete floor as I sat down next to her, either. She was reading a paperback, but I could tell by the way her shoulders hunched that the reason she wasn't looking up had nothing to do with her book.

"Hi," I said. "What are you reading?"

She held up the paperback for a millisecond, long enough for me to see the word *Boyfriend* in the title. Then she turned back to her book until Ms. Rusgo called for our attention.

"Hello, hello," she said in her usual energized voice. "Today we're going to work on something fun. We're going to use clay to create original pinch pots!"

While Ms. Rusgo demonstrated how to shape the clay to form pots, my mind raced with ideas. "There's no such thing as a right or wrong way to create pottery," Ms. Rusgo continued. "If you don't like the way your pot is shaping up, feel free to start over. But remember, some of the most amazing art has been made because of the imperfections. You might think it's lopsided; someone else will look at it and only see the beauty and originality in your creation."

I got to work right away, almost forgetting Jessie was nearby until I heard her pounding her clay next to me. Ms. Rusgo stopped at our table. "Jessie. Oh, Jessie!" Ms. Rusgo leaned over and put an arm around her. "I sense some frustration in the way you're approaching this project. There's no need to pound . . . use your fingers instead of your fist to work with the clay, to knead it like dough. There now, that's much better," she said as Jessie began rolling the dough back and forth on the table.

"Come on, chin up!" Ms. Rusgo said cheerily before she came around to my side. "You can do this, Jessie."

"Now, Sunny, this is wonderful! I sense that you and the clay are working together instead of against each other. I can't wait to see what you come up with."

Jessie kicked her foot against the table leg and smushed all the clay back together in a ball.

"Do you want some help?" I whispered.

She dropped the clay on the table and turned to face me. "I saw you yesterday."

I swallowed. "Yesterday?"

"You were sitting out front with that red-haired girl."

"Lydia?" Why couldn't Jessie at least use her name?

"Yeah, Lydia Applehead, or whatever she's called—"

"Applebaum. Her name's Lydia Applebaum."

"Whatever. Anyway, I thought you had an appointment after school."

My mind raced. Two years of Odyssey of the Mind should have made me a quick thinker. Where were my spontaneous skills when I needed them?

"You admit you lied to me, then?" Jessie asked, her voice getting louder. A couple of kids turned around to stare at us.

Ms. Rusgo called out, "Shhh, shhh, quiet work produces creative expression."

"No," I lied, again. Going back to my original lie sounded better than making up a new one. "My appointment was super quick. At the orthodontist. He checked my teeth to see if I needed braces, and then he let us go. Mom said I could come back for the rest of the OM meeting. I mean, I didn't want to walk in on Drama Club late when I'd never been before."

Jessie was studying me carefully through narrowed eyes, but I could tell she was thinking about what I'd said, wondering if I was telling her the truth.

"Plus, I didn't know where Drama Club was meeting, so I went to OM."

Jessie stared at me a minute longer, then went back to rolling her clay back and forth on the table. At least she wasn't pounding it, which I took as a positive sign.

After a little while, Jessie asked, "Do you need them?"

I looked up at her. "Need what?"

"Braces? Isn't that what you went to the orthodontist for?"

"Oh, that. Yeah." I showed her my teeth. You couldn't ignore evidence like that.

Jessie nodded and turned back to her clay and we worked quietly for the rest of the class. When the bell rang, she picked up her backpack and headed out of the room without waiting, like she usually did.

I couldn't let her get away. If I didn't sit with her today, it would be like a door closing . . . One that wouldn't open again.

"Hey, Jessie!" I called out. "Wait up!"

She stopped at the doorway.

"You're not still mad at me, are you?" I asked as I fell in step beside her. "I mean, because it's not my fault I had an orthodontist appointment—"

"I've decided I'm not going out for Drama Club," Jessie said. "I've already got too much going on since I'm on a dance team and I'll have cheerleading practice soon. Plus, none of my friends are joining."

"Oh," I said, feeling like I'd just dropped my heavy backpack in the middle of the hallway and I could move twice as fast. Now I didn't have to worry about coming up with an excuse again next week. "That's great—I mean, it sounds like you're really busy."

"Yeah." Jessie didn't say anything until we were almost at the cafeteria. Then she stopped and turned to face me. "Just don't do that again."

I gave her a puzzled look.

"Lie to me. I need to trust my friends, and I don't like liars."

When I stood there, frozen to the spot, she grabbed me by the wrist. "Come on, Sunny. The others will be wondering where we are."

Stung by Jessie's words, I followed her to the lunch table, where I stayed quiet until the bell rang for fourth period.

CHAPTER FOURTEEN

The rest of September flew by. Once we'd settled on the problem, our OM team got straight to work brainstorming ideas for the skit. Thanks to Avi and his out-of-space ideas, our main character was going to be Annalise Alien, and we had an awesome idea for our solution. Lydia still barely looked at me during practices, but when I made suggestions she didn't shoot them down.

As for Jessie, she was still talking to me during art class and letting me sit with her crowd during lunch, but our friendship seemed to have skidded to a stop after I'd lied about the appointment, and I didn't know what to do about it. Sunny's Super-Stupendous Plan for Getting Mom and Dad Back Together seemed to have hit a lot of dead ends as well. I was like a car spinning its wheels in the mud, trying different things but going nowhere.

That's why I found myself doing something on the first Monday in October that I never thought I'd have the nerve to do. As soon as Jessie sat down next to me at the art table, I said, "You want to come over after school some day this week?"

Jessie looked at me with an expression on her face I couldn't read. Was she trying to think fast to come up with an excuse like I had done when I didn't want to go to the Drama Club meeting with her?

Then she shrugged. "Okay," she said, pulling a datebook out of her backpack. "I can do Friday. Why don't you come over to my house instead? Mom can pick us up."

"Yeah, sure," I said, letting out a deep breath. Jessie snapped her planner shut and tossed it back in her backpack. I was excited. This was my chance to work on two problems at once—fixing my friendship with Jessie and planning Mom's makeover. With Jessie's expert fashion advice, Mom was sure to look like a model by the time we were through.

***

"You have a really nice house," I told Jessie as we sat in her huge, open kitchen Friday afternoon. It was as clean as Grandma Grace's, with shiny, uncluttered countertops.

"It's okay," Jessie said with a shrug. "The best part is the basement. We have a Ping-Pong table, video games, stuff like that."

"Wow. Do you have brothers or sisters?"

"Nope, just me and Mom."

I wanted to ask her about her dad, but didn't want to sound nosy. Her parents could be divorced, or her dad could have died . . . or she could even have a strange situation like me.

"What about you?" Jessie asked. "Do you have any brothers or sisters?"

"I have a sister in third grade."

"Why'd you move down here from New Jersey?"

I tucked a strand of hair behind my ear. "My mom wanted to go back to school, so we came down here to stay with my grandmother."

"Did your dad move in with your grandma, too?"

I paused. "Actually, he's still in New Jersey."

"So your parents are splitting up. Well, don't worry. It'll be okay. My mom and dad used to fight all the time. Now it's a lot better."

"Really? When did your parents get divorced?"

"About two years ago. Dad has a new girlfriend. A really *young* girlfriend."

"That stinks."

Jessie took a sip from her water bottle. "I don't see him that often, but whenever I do, he buys me everything I want. It's not that bad."

"My parents aren't splitting up, though. They get along pretty well."

"Then why didn't your dad come with you?"

I looked down at my clementine, concentrating on pulling apart the sections carefully. "He couldn't leave his store. We're going back in two years, when Mom finishes her degree."

"That's how it starts," Jessie said, a knowing edge to her voice. "They try to act like everything's okay, but who do they think they're fooling? Mom and Dad used to fight so much I was almost *relieved* when they finally told me they were getting a divorce."

"My parents never fight. They're best friends," I said, though I wasn't sure that was true anymore. Best friends talked to each other. Best friends wanted to spend time together, and live in the same state, at least.

Jessie didn't say anything more, but she raised one eyebrow like she didn't believe a word I was saying. I'd told her all I wanted to about Mom and Scott, and I certainly didn't plan to share that I was adopted—but only by Mom—so I picked up a piece of popcorn, tossed it in the air, and caught it in my mouth. Then I tossed two pieces and caught those, too.

"Bet you can't catch three," Jessie finally said.

"Bet you can't catch *one*."

Jessie tossed a piece in the air and it landed on her nose. I giggled.

"Give me a chance," she said, and after a few more tries she got the hang of it.

Soon we were both up to threes, popcorn littered the kitchen floor, and we were making so much noise that Mrs. Landers came in to check on us. "Girls, what in the world is going on in here?"

I took one look at Jessie's mom standing there with her hand on one hip, and I stopped tossing and giggling. I wondered if I'd messed up any chance of being invited back. I kicked the pile of popcorn under my feet.

"It's okay, Mom. No big deal," Jessie said. "We'll clean up."

Mrs. Landers gave Jessie a harsh look, then glanced over at me. "Don't forget to use a broom. I don't know how you managed it, but there's popcorn all over the kitchen floor."

"No problem, Mom," Jessie said. Mrs. Landers hesitated, then shook her head and left the room. As soon as she was gone, Jessie burst out laughing and tossed a handful of popcorn in the air. I laughed, too, but I knew Mrs. Landers had put an official end to the contest. We finished what was left in the bowl, picked up what we could find, then headed upstairs without sweeping. Grandma Grace would have had a fit if we left her kitchen like that. But I figured if Jessie didn't think we needed to clean up, I sure wasn't going to insist on it.

Jessie's room was super neat like the rest of the house. I sat down on her bed, not surprised to see the comforter with its peace sign and smiley-face pattern. Her bulletin board was full of photos, and a few posters of movie stars and pop stars were hung on the walls.

"I like your room," I said.

"Thanks. So what do you want to do now? We could go down to the basement and play Ping-Pong, or we could watch some YouTube videos?"

"How about a makeover?" I said, not wanting to waste any more time. "I mean, since you know a lot about fashion—"

"Oh, that would be awesome!" Jessie's eyes lit up. "I was thinking you could use a little help, but I didn't want to hurt your feelings."

My cheeks flamed. "Um, well," I managed to say as my hand flew to my hair. "My hair's kind of in that in-between stage."

"Oh, don't worry about that," Jessie said, opening her top dresser drawer. It had enough little bottles and containers to fill a cosmetics factory. "We can start with your face, and then we'll straighten up your hair, okay?"

I got up to take a closer look. "Where did you get all this stuff?"

"It's a hobby. Mom doesn't mind. She lets me wear it."

I glanced at Jessie's face. Most of her eyeliner had worn off, though her eyelids still sparkled with a little blue shadow. "You don't use *all* this stuff, do you?"

Jessie shrugged. "I could, if I wanted to. For a fancy occasion or something. I like to experiment. Come on, let me show you. Just for fun."

I wasn't sure how I was going to get back into the house with my face all made-up, but I knew the sacrifice would be worth it. Jessie seemed so excited about the opportunity to transform me that I was sure she'd forgotten all about my little lie a couple of weeks ago. Maybe our friendship could finally gain some momentum. Even more importantly, if she had fun doing my makeover, I wouldn't have any trouble convincing her to use her skills and talent on transforming my mom.

"Okay," I said. "Where would you like me to sit?"

***

I stared into the mirror a while later, unable to take my eyes off my reflection. "Wow," I said. Black liner made my eyes look huge, like a cat's, and I'd chosen the same sparkly blue shadow and mascara that Jessie was wearing. She'd brushed pink powder on my cheekbones and used one of her tinted lip balms to make my lips shiny. Not only that, Jessie had trimmed a few scraggly strands of hair and used the flat iron to make it look straight and smooth. "I look like a different person!"

"You could pass for sixteen," Jessie said.

"Sixteen?" My eyes opened wide. "Really?"

"Well . . . fourteen, at least. You should wear your hair this way to school. You look amazing."

"Thanks." I turned around to face her, and the words just came rushing out. "Hey, do you think you could do a makeover for my mom?"

Jessie laughed. "Your mom wants a makeover?"

I shrugged. "I don't know if she wants one, exactly . . . but I thought it would make a good photo. To send to my dad."

Jessie thought about it for a minute. Then she smiled. "I'd love to help. That's what friends are for, right?"

SUNNY'S SUPER-STUPENDOUS PLAN TO GET MOM AND DAD BACK TOGETHER

1. Tell Scott that Mom has heavy bags under her eyes from crying so much, and to please send the Eezy Breezy Sleep Mask or a pound of cucumbers. Hasn't sent anything yet. **Sent cukes with dressing. He totally doesn't get it.**

2. Ask Mom to send Scott a pair of suspenders. Tell her that he has already lost four pounds because he's too sad to eat, and his jeans keep falling down. Mom laughed when I told her this. She said, "Don't you worry. Scott knows how to take care of himself. I bet he's living it up, eating at a different restaurant every night. Gained four pounds is probably more like it!"

3. Put up photos of Scott all over the house: on the refrigerator, on Mom's desk, on top of Mom's dresser, and on the bathroom mirror. Mom is too busy to notice. I asked her if she saw the photo on the bathroom mirror. She didn't even look up from her laptop. Just said, "Mmm-hmm," and kept right on typing.

4. Find glamorous photos of Mom and send them to Scott. Haven't found any yet. Mom is wearing old jeans with her hair pulled back in all the

photos I've looked at. Will have to think about this one more. **Jessie's going to help! We may be on to something here!**

5. Send flowers to Mom from "A Secret Admirer." This will make Scott jealous enough to change his mind about letting Mom move so far away. It made Mom start talking about old boyfriends, which was totally disgusting. And Scott just laughed about the whole thing. UGH.

6. Make a playlist of Scott's favorite love songs—the mushier, the better! Be sure to blast it in the house and in the car every time you get in. Make a playlist of Mom's favorite love songs and send it to Scott. Time to get started on this one. **Made the play-list and play it around Mom every chance I get. Mom always sings along. She is probably thinking of Scott while she sings, so this may be working! Scott thanked me for the playlist but hasn't said anything to Mom about it yet (as far as I know).**

7. Ask Mom to make Scott's Manicotti Special. At the table, take a bite, sigh, and say, "It just doesn't taste the same without Scott here to share it." Mom's too busy with classes. Grandma Grace does all the cooking. Maybe I should cook it?

8. Ask Mom about the old days, when she and Scott first fell in love. Ask Scott the same thing. Haven't gotten around to it yet! **Unfortunately, Mom seems to have a bad memory. Or could it be that she doesn't want to share her memories with me?**

9. ~~Bake Mom's special mint Oreo pie and send it to Scott. Put a card inside the box that says "Made for you, with love from Rebecca."~~ How do you send ice cream pie through the mail?

10. Ask Grandma Grace for a chore list to earn some extra money. Buy a gift certificate for Mom and Scott to a fancy Italian restaurant. Make sure it has candlelight, wine, and spaghetti for two, just like in *Lady and the Tramp.* Give them the gift certificate when Scott comes to visit at Christmas time (or sooner). Haven't asked Grandma Grace yet—she doesn't seem like the type who will actually pay me for chores.

11. Enter one of those Perfect Family contests. When Mom and Scott see the winning entry, they'll realize how much they belong together. Not only that, but the whole family wins a trip to Disney World! Looked in Grandma Grace's magazines but I haven't seen any contest listings.

12. ~~Enter the "Perfect Husband" contest. Tell all about how Scott would make a perfect husband for Mom and wait for your entry to be published, then show it to Mom. Enter the "Perfect Wife" contest and send the winning published entry to send Scott.~~ I've been looking for this kind of contest and all I can find is one called "The Perfect Man" or "The Perfect Woman." The winner gets to choose the eligible bachelor or bachelorette of his or her choice.

13. Convince Mom she needs a makeover. Buy her a red shirt because "studies show that both genders are more attracted to people when they wear red." Snap her photo afterward and send it to Scott in a sparkly frame with hearts around the border. Jessie's going to do the makeover! I've already made the perfect frame.

14. Make a photo album with lots of pictures of Mom and Scott when they were young and in love. Include a few pictures of Autumn and me to show how we glued them together as one big family. Give it to Mom on her birthday. Having a bit of trouble finding photos of just the two of them. Have asked Scott to look through his stack of photos since Mom is not the least bit sentimental.

CHAPTER FIFTEEN

On Saturday, we met for our first Odyssey of the Mind practice at Lydia's. With all the props and set-building to be done, we'd need to meet some weekends to finish everything on time, and it would have to be at someone's house whose parents didn't mind if the team made a huge mess. Lydia had been the first to offer her basement.

Mom dropped me off before another "critique" date with Jeb. They were going to be meeting at the coffee shop.

"I'll pick you up at three o'clock," Mom said when she pulled into Lydia's driveway.

I grabbed my notebook and folder, then took another glance at my mom. She was wearing her hair loose, curls tumbling over her shoulders. She also had on a light-blue fitted shirt instead of her usual baggy T-shirt. "Why aren't you wearing a ponytail?" I asked.

"Oh, I just needed a change." Mom glanced away from me and started fiddling with the radio.

Things were getting more and more disastrous by the minute. I needed to do something, and quick, so I reached for Mom's phone and snapped a photo.

"Sunny?" Mom blinked at me. "What are you doing?"

"Um, well, you look so nice that I wanted to take a picture."

Mom ran a hand across her hair and smiled. "Thanks."

I stared at her a minute longer, then said, "Don't be late!" before slamming the door for emphasis. When I got home, I was going to send that photo to Scott with a message: *Mom's dressing up like* this *to go out with a guy. Thought you should know!*

Jeb was probably one of those writer types who wore a stylish cap and had a jacket with patches on the elbows. I bet he drank his coffee super black, no sugar.

Scott liked lots of sugar and milk in his coffee. Whipped cream if he could get away with it. And the only caps he wore had words on them, like MYSTIC BEACH.

I closed my eyes and squeezed them tight, trying to wipe the picture of Jeb out of my mind just as Mrs. Applebaum opened the door.

"Hi Sunny!" she greeted me. "Come on in. Everyone's downstairs."

Lydia's house looked a lot like our home in New Jersey. Comfy. Sunlight poured through large windows in the living room where every empty space was covered: coffee mugs and magazines on the table, shoes scattered across the floor, blankets and pillows on the sofa, a cat on the recliner.

Her house had an interesting smell, too, like oatmeal cookies baking in the oven mixed with incense burning in another room.

I stopped to pet the tabby curled up on the chair, feeling that familiar ache of missing my own cat. "What's his name?"

"Aristotle. Einstein and Copernicus are wandering around here somewhere." Mrs. Applebaum smiled at me. "By the way, feel free to call me Darlene."

"Okay," I said, though I didn't think I would. Lydia and I were barely on speaking terms, and I'd feel funny calling her mom by her first name, as if we were best friends.

I headed down the stairs to the basement. Everyone else was already there. Green carpet covered part of the concrete floor, which had been painted in rainbow colors. An old sofa that looked like it was being used as a cat scratching post sat against one wall. Drawers with all kinds of art supplies lined the other wall. There weren't any windows, but posters like the ones at the health food store brightened up the room.

I sat down next to Jalia on the sofa while Coach Baker led a brainstorming session, writing down our thoughts on chart paper. Then we broke into groups to start on the scenery. A couple of kids were putting together PVC piping for a stand, and a few others were trying to decide how to make a 3-D spaceship. I wandered over to Lydia and Jalia, who were on the floor sketching out the first scene.

"Can I help?" I asked.

"Sure!" Jalia said before Lydia could say anything, so I sat down on the floor next to them.

"Have you ever seen *Hamlet*?" I asked as I helped roll out the white paper we'd use for the backdrop. "I don't know a thing about Shakespeare. Except that he was writing a long time ago."

"Mom took me to see *Macbeth*," Lydia said. "But I didn't understand much of it."

"I thought you were a big Shakespeare fan," I said. "You're the one who really wanted this problem, right?"

"I wanted to do musical theater. It sounded like fun."

"So you don't know anything about Shakespeare, either?" Jalia asked her.

"Nope."

Jalia put down her pencil and sat straight up. "Am I the only one on the whole team who's seen the plays?"

"Probably," Lydia said without looking up.

Jalia heaved a big sigh.

"It doesn't matter," Lydia said. "To Be or Not to Be is a skit about a character realizing the easy way out isn't always the best choice. We're supposed to use our imaginations, remember?"

Jalia pushed her glasses back up on her nose. "Well, sure. But the winning team's going to be one that uses lots of Shakespeare puns and references in their skit."

"So that's where you'll come in handy," Lydia said. "Besides, the rest of us can do some research. All you have to do is use the Internet and type in 'Shakespeare quotes.' I bet we'll have way more than we know what to do with."

"Hey, that's a great idea," I said. Lydia didn't respond to me, but I could tell she looked pleased by my compliment.

Jalia sighed again, but then she got back down on her stomach to work.

An hour later, our forest scene was starting to take shape. "Not bad," Lydia said, sitting up and looking over the backdrop. "You're pretty good at this, Sunny."

"Thanks." It was the first nice thing Lydia had said to me in a while, so I breathed it in and let her words fill me up.

"Mom says we can meet here again next week," Lydia told Coach Baker. "We've got tons of paint and art supplies."

"Excellent!" Coach Baker said. "Team handshake, everyone!" We gathered around and put our hands on top of one another's, one at a time, the way we always did at the end of a meeting. "Good job today, guys!" Coach Baker said as we pulled our hands away and gave ourselves a round of applause.

As I put away art supplies, I noticed a stack of flyers on top of a cabinet—the same ones that had been posted on the bulletin board at Earthly Goods.

The animal rights meeting, the one about Fur-Free Friday, was two weeks away. Mom had said not to confront Grandma Grace about animal rights, but as I picked up the flyer and stuck it in my pocket, I realized something important. If I went to the meeting and helped make signs for the protest, it didn't mean anyone had to find out.

CHAPTER SIXTEEN

From: MadelineL@ilovebooks.com
To: SunnyKid@CreativityisCool.com
What's New?

I haven't heard from you in a while! How's your musical coming along? We started working on putting the car together. So far there's been a lot of arguing. Plus, I hammered my finger last week and my nail is turning purple. OWW! Maybe I should have picked musical theater instead.

Carmen Santelli invited me to her sleepover this weekend. I'm not really friends with her, but she's inviting almost all the sixth-grade girls. I heard she has a huge basement!

Wish you could come, too.
Maddy

From: SunnyKid@CreativityisCool.com
To: MadelineL@ilovebooks.com
Re: What's New?

We have a pretty good team here. We're doing things a little backward, starting on the set before we've written the script. But we've come up with a storyboard and the coach seems to know what he's doing since he's taken a team to Worlds before!

Have you seen Stellaluna lately? I know Scott takes good care of her, but it's good for her to hear a girl's voice.

I've been feeding this stray cat that comes around every once in a while, but I haven't told Grandma Grace. Her name is Ripple.

Sunny

P.S. When did you change your name to Maddy?

***

"What are you doing this weekend?" I asked Jessie in art class on Monday. "Can you come over to do Mom's makeover?"

She pulled out her planner. "I've got dance class Saturday morning, a sleepover Saturday night, and youth group Sunday evening. I can come over on Sunday, from one to three. You better warn your mom."

"Really? That would be great. But I haven't asked her about it yet. Mom can be stubborn about things . . ."

"Don't worry," Jessie said. "We'll come up with something. Now, what's your address?"

I scribbled it down on a piece of paper and handed it to her, hoping Jessie was right.

***

Before I knew it, Sunday had arrived and I hadn't done a thing to prepare my mom. Luckily, she didn't have a meeting with Jeb or a long lunch date planned with old friends, and she said she'd be home all afternoon. But I had no idea how we were going to pull it off.

The doorbell rang at exactly one o'clock. Jessie was dressed for the occasion in a short skirt and ruffled top, and I could tell she'd taken extra care with her makeup for a Sunday afternoon.

"You look great," I told her as she walked inside.

"Thanks, Sunny." She spotted my mom at the table in front of her laptop. "You know I always feel better when I look my best," she said loudly.

I bit my lip to keep from bursting out laughing. If this was Jessie's plan, I figured I'd let her run with it. Jessie walked right over to my mom and said, "Hello, Mrs. Beringer. I'm Jessie Landers. It's very nice to meet you!"

Mom looked up from her computer and smiled. "Hi, Jessie. I'm glad that you could come over today. Well, you girls have fun," she said, waving us up the stairs.

Jessie didn't move from her spot. She looked over at me as if to say, *You were right. She's going to be a tough one.* Then she put her bag down on the chair next to my mom with a loud clunk. "Actually, Mrs. Beringer, we were hoping you might help us with a project."

"Sunny didn't mention a project." Mom logged off her computer and closed the top. Then she turned toward us. "How can I help?"

"Well," Jessie said, clearing her throat and glancing over at me, "this is actually my project, not Sunny's. See, I'm taking a modeling class. And we're learning how to do our hair and makeup correctly—"

"I have to say that you've done a great job with it," Mom said. "But aren't you a little young to be worrying about hair and makeup?"

"You're never too young to take pride in your appearance," Jessie said, opening her bag and placing a stand-up mirror on the table. "Our instructor says, 'You're never too old, either.'"

I choked back a giggle and ended up making a noise between a snort and a cough.

"You okay, Sunny?" Mom asked.

I nodded. "I think you should help Jessie with her project."

Mom hesitated, then said, "Okay. What do I need to do?"

"Great!" Jessie said, clapping her hands. She began laying out her supplies: little containers of shadows and powders, mascara, a flat iron, a hair brush. "We're supposed to practice on an adult so we can learn proper technique."

"Oh, no." Mom shook her head. "You're going to put all this stuff on *me?*"

"It won't take long," Jessie said. "Ms. Lee says that doing your hair and makeup is a fine art, and that we need to practice on others. We have to take pictures of everyone we do makeovers on. Sunny said you wouldn't mind."

Mom raised her eyebrow at me.

"Come on, Mom, it'll be fun! Oh, and you need to change into this," I said, handing her a gift bag. Jessie had picked out a red shirt for Mom at the mall with her Frequent Shopper Discount Card.

Mom pulled out the shirt, then looked up at me. "Red is not exactly my color, you know."

"Sorry, it's part of my assignment," Jessie said quickly.

Mom hesitated. "Oh, all right." She picked up the shirt and scooted out of the room.

I looked over at Jessie and grinned. I couldn't believe my mom actually fell for our plan. "Ooh, red *is* so your color," Jessie said when Mom returned with a shirt that fit her perfectly. I watched as Jessie got to work, expertly applying creams and powders, the same way she had with me.

When Autumn came into the kitchen and sat down and watched the transformation, her mouth dropped open. Mom sat perfectly still the whole time and didn't complain once, not even when Jessie straightened her curls with a flat iron.

Maybe she was thinking it was time for a change, too. Hopefully, she wasn't paying too close attention. The last thing I needed was for Mom to look this good for a "critique date" with Jeb.

"Taa-daa!" Jessie said, reaching for a mirror a few minutes later.

"Wow, Mom," I said, "you look fantastic!"

"Like a fashion model!" Autumn chimed in.

Mom peered at her reflection, running a hand over her straight, glossy hair. "I have to admit, I certainly look different."

"You look very glamorous, Mrs. Beringer," Jessie said. "I'll get a good grade on this makeover."

"Say cheese!" I said, picking up my camera. I snapped a few shots to be safe. I couldn't wait to hear what Scott had to say when he saw her picture. It was sure to bring love back into his eyes, and I had Jessie, my new friend, to thank for it.

***

A packet of photos arrived from Scott the following week. I ran up to my room and opened the envelope, shaking out a pile of pictures onto my bed. A folded piece of paper fell out, too, and I read the note:

Dear Sunflower,

I found this envelope of photos in my drawer. Hope this helps. Luckily, the dates were already marked on the backs or I'd have no idea when these were taken! Good luck with your project!

Love,
Scott

I sifted through the photos, looking for that special one that would remind Mom how much they were in love. The first photo I picked up showed a picture of the two of them in front of a college sign. Mom's hair was in a long braid that hung over one shoulder. Scott's hair covered his ears and almost reached his shoulders. They both wore jeans and T-shirts and they were grinning as if they might burst out laughing at any minute.

There were a couple more of them together, but mostly, it was photos of them with groups of friends, including Scott's twin brother, Mark. Mark died in a car crash when I was little and Scott didn't talk about him much. They sure looked a lot alike.

I studied the photos closely, but I didn't see any where Mom and Scott were gazing into each other's eyes. They looked like they were having a great time . . . but they looked mostly like good friends.

These photos were not going to make Mom remember how she was once madly in love. My album was going to be a total flop.

I sifted through the pile again, wondering if I'd missed something. Nothing. Not even a glimpse. I was getting nowhere, and Mom's birthday was only a couple of weeks away.

I heaved a big sigh. Then I piled up the photos and dropped them back in the envelope. But as my fingers dropped against one of them, it felt thicker than the others. I stopped and took a closer look. A photo was stuck on the back, so I peeled it off.

The photo dropped facedown on the bed. *Rebecca, Mark, and Sunflower* was scribbled in Scott's handwriting. The date written below the names was my birthday.

My heart pounded as I flipped it over. I was holding the photo of Mom and Scott and me in the delivery room right after I was born. Only it wasn't Scott who was leaning in and staring down at me with love.

CHAPTER SEVENTEEN

I pulled my hand away quickly, as if I'd touched a hot stove.

Why was *Mark* holding me in the hospital after I was born, and why did he have his arm around Mom?

I stood up, shoving my chair hard against the desk. Then I stomped back and forth across the floor, trying to put the pieces together. Mom had acted weird when she'd seen that photo on the computer, like there was something she needed to tell me. But she never said a word. She just acted like it was Scott in the photo, like they were a mom and dad holding their newborn in the hospital.

Mom and Scott never talked about Mark, and here he was holding me? It didn't make any sense. Now that I thought about it, there was something strange about the fact that Scott never talked about his twin brother. I'd always figured it made him too sad, but now I wondered if there was more to the story.

A fireball burned in the pit of my stomach. Parents weren't supposed to lie to their children. They weren't supposed to keep secrets, and they weren't supposed to act like things were one way when the truth was totally different.

Maybe Scott and Mom had gotten away with it for eleven years and ten months. But that didn't mean I was going to let them get away with it for one day longer.

I yanked the bedroom door open and marched downstairs. When I got to the kitchen, Mom was in her usual spot, typing away on her laptop. All my noise hadn't even put a dent in her concentration.

I stood behind her for a moment, taking deep breaths, wondering when she was going to notice me. Finally, I dropped the photo right on top of the keyboard.

There. That should get her attention.

"Sunny?" Mom's fingers slipped off the keys. "What's going on?"

"Maybe you should be telling me," I said, proud that my voice came out strong and steady.

Mom picked up the photo and studied it for a moment. "Where did this come from?"

"Scott sent it. You're the one who told me to ask him for old photos for my project, remember? Well, that's one of the ones he sent. Go ahead, look at the back."

Mom flipped it over and stared at the writing. Not that she needed to. She knew perfectly well what it would say.

"Why did you lie to me? You said it was Scott holding me."

Mom didn't reply. She flipped the photo back to the other side and stared at it, as if the photo might hold all the answers.

I dropped down onto the chair next to her and crossed my arms in front of my chest. "I'm waiting."

"Oh, honey," Mom finally said. "I've been wanting to talk to you about this for a long time. I never wanted you to find out this way."

"There's not much you can do about that now." I kicked my foot against the table leg. "You said we needed to move to Bennetsville because you needed a change. But now I'm wondering what else you haven't told me."

Mom let out a long sigh. Then she nodded, snapping her laptop shut. She sat there for a moment, like she was trying to figure out the right thing to say.

Just spit it out already! I wanted to yell at her. Instead, I sat there, drumming my fingernails against the tabletop.

"Okay," Mom finally said. "I guess I should start at the beginning. Back when I first met Scott . . . and Mark, in college."

"I always thought you and Scott had been dating since college. I guess you were lying about that, too."

"Now hold on a minute," Mom said. "I told you we *met* in college. I never said we started dating right away—"

"Same thing. You were lying. About that *and* the photo."

"Scott and I did go out a couple of times in college." Mom must have decided she was suddenly thirsty, because she got up to pour herself a tall glass of water. Then she sat back down, swallowing half of it in large gulps.

"And?"

"And . . . as I got to know Mark better, we fell in love."

"And you just forgot to tell me?"

"It didn't seem like something you needed to know. Past history, and all that."

"What happened next?"

Mom continued talking, telling me how she and Mark dated for years after college, how they talked about getting married, but she wanted to have children and Mark didn't.

"Then what?" I interrupted. "If he didn't want kids, why was he holding me in the hospital?"

"He changed his mind."

"About having kids?"

Mom's eyes were shining when she nodded. "He moved in with me a few weeks after you were born to help out, and he fell in love with you. We started talking again about getting married, about putting his name on the adoption papers . . . and then, when you were three months old, he was killed in a car crash."

Silence filled the space between us. Mom took another swig of her water.

"Is that when you started dating Scott again? Right after Mark died?"

Mom shook her head slowly. "Scott and I were friends— best friends like we'd always been. He stepped right in to help out when you were a baby, like he was your dad even though he didn't live with us. And a couple of years later, when I decided to adopt Autumn, he was right there with me, even if his name wasn't on the adoption papers."

"But you were a couple when you adopted Autumn, right?"

"We dated on and off . . ."

"And then what?"

"We tried, Sunny. We really did, until you were about ten."

Mom's words were spinning like a tornado in my head. "You're always saying me and Autumn should tell the truth. But you've been lying to us this whole time."

Mom shook her head. "Not the whole time. We dated for a while—"

"You didn't tell me the whole truth." I balled my hands into fists, clenching so tightly that my nails dug into my skin. Two years. Two *whole* years! And, even before that, they had tried "on and off," always pretending they were a couple and like they'd been together forever. Nothing about Mom and Scott was the way it seemed. Nothing! I stood up and slammed my chair against the table. "How could you do it? You never told me about Mark, you lied about the photo, you lied to me about everything!"

"Oh, Sunny," Mom said. "We never meant to hurt you. This doesn't change anything."

"It changes *everything*!" I yelled as I stormed out of the room.

"Sunny, please." Mom started up the steps behind me, but I raced to my room, slamming the door behind me. I heard her footsteps stop outside the door. There was a long pause, as if she was trying to figure out what to do next. She didn't knock or call out again, and soon I heard her footsteps fade away as she headed down the hall.

I threw myself down on the bed. Everything Mom had told me swirled around inside, faster and faster. I tried to make my mind blank. I pictured a calm lake, but tidal waves kept taking over the image in my mind.

Why had my mom adopted me anyway, when she knew she couldn't count on a dad to help? Was she lonely, and only thinking of herself? Maybe this was why she kept that quote above her desk, "To thine own self be true." Maybe it only meant that she was thinking about herself above everyone else.

As I thought more about it, I tried to figure out why she adopted a second baby when she was so mixed up about who she wanted to be with. Didn't she ever stop to think that children needed two parents who were committed to staying together?

And what about Scott? If he loved me the way he said he did, why wasn't his name on those adoption papers?

Now, there was nothing linking Mom and Dad and me and Autumn together.

I felt like someone had pushed me out of a spaceship and I was floating around in the atmosphere, nothing tying me to Earth.

A little while later, there was a knock on my door. "Sunny? Scott's on the phone. He wants to talk to you."

I didn't get up. "Tell him I don't feel like talking."

"Come on, honey." Mom's voice was soft. "Please open the door." I didn't answer. I didn't move.

Unfortunately, Grandma Grace didn't believe in locks, so Mom opened the door. "I know how upset you are," she said, sitting down next to me on the bed. "If you won't talk to me, then you should talk to Scott. He feels terrible about everything."

"I'm not talking," I said again. Then I rolled over and faced the wall.

Mom squeezed my shoulder. "Tomorrow, then?"

I shrugged.

"She'll talk tomorrow, Scott," Mom said into the phone. "Okay . . . sure . . . I'll tell her. All right, bye." Mom turned to me. "Scott said to tell you he loves you. And I love you, too. You know that, right?"

I shrugged again.

"Things will look better in the morning." Mom's voice had taken on a fake-cheery tone. She rose and left the room, closing the door quietly behind her.

A few minutes later, I got up, pulling my notebook out of the drawer. I stared down at "Sunny's Super-Stupendous Plan to Get Mom and Dad Back Together." What a joke.

I tore out the pages, ripping them into little pieces. They fluttered their way into the trash can, my totally awesome plan destroyed with a single photo, along with my dreams of the family I thought I had.

CHAPTER EIGHTEEN

Hot, fresh cinnamon rolls, coming right up!" Grandma Grace said, putting a plate full of rolls on the table as I made my way into the kitchen the next morning.

I glanced over at my grandmother, then at my mom. Grandma Grace never made breakfast for us during the week, and we never had something fancy like cinnamon rolls.

"Mmm, yumm!" Autumn said, bouncing up and down in her seat. "Wow, thanks, Grandma!"

I watched as my sister reached for a warm roll, licking the icing off her fingers.

"Your grandmother thought you might need a special treat this morning," Mom said, squeezing my shoulder.

I shrugged away her hand. Did Mom really think that a special breakfast would make everything better between us? A cinnamon roll was certainly not going to change the fact that Mom and Scott had lied to me all my life, and that my whole reality had shifted.

"Ooh, my favorite!" Autumn said, taking a bite.

I shot my mom a dirty look. I couldn't believe she had told my grandmother about the photo. The last thing I needed was for Grandma Grace to be nosing around in our family business. That was private, between me and Mom and Scott. The only other person Mom needed to tell was Autumn, but it was clear she hadn't said a word to her.

"Well, I'm not hungry," I said, getting up from the table.

"What's wrong?" Autumn asked as I left the room. "I thought you loved cinnamon rolls, Sunny!"

I just shook my head without looking at any of them. The sugary sweet smell made my stomach rumble, but as I thought about the photo I was only left with a bitter taste in my mouth.

***

"Methinks Mom and Scott have been practicing the art of deception," I told Ripple in the yard after the OM meeting Wednesday afternoon. Jalia had brought in one of Shakespeare's plays and we all had to sit there and watch it for fifteen minutes, "no matter how much you moan and groan," Coach Baker had said. He told us it was important for us to hear the way the characters spoke so we could work some of the language into our script.

Turns out the language was kind of fun to play around with. I ran my hand over Ripple's fur. She'd been showing up more often, waiting for me. Maybe the other people had stopped feeding her. Or maybe, just maybe, she'd decided she was mine.

I stood up and put my hand over my heart. "Something is rotten in the state of Denmark!" Ripple purred as she rubbed up against me.

"Okay, not Denmark exactly. That's just a Shakespeare quote that Lydia pulled up. But something is definitely fishy in the state of North Carolina. Can you believe Mom and Scott have been lying to me? I don't trust either of them.

"I'm madder at Mom than I am at Scott, but that's just because this is all her fault. It wasn't Scott's idea to split up the family." Ripple rolled over on her belly and let me scratch her under her chin.

"But I'm mad at Scott, too." Scott had called every night since I found out about the photo, but I'd refused to talk to him. What was the point? He wouldn't be able to tell me anything different. I knew not talking to me was killing him, but I didn't care. Let him feel awful, just like I did.

"He lied to me just like Mom did. Plus, he never signed my adoption papers, so what does that tell you?" Ripple stretched and purred. She was a pretty good listener as long as I kept petting her. I told her the whole story. Ripple didn't have any advice, so after she finished off the plate of tuna I got up and went inside.

I sat at my desk staring at my math assignment for a while, not doing any of the problems. My math teacher, Mr. Lioni, always told us that the good thing about math is you can't argue with logic. If you did the problems right, you got the right answer.

Not like real life, where sometimes things didn't add up and everyone came to different conclusions. I closed my eyes for a minute, trying to sort it all out. Snapshots formed in my mind: Mom, Dad, Autumn, and me . . . laughing and hugging, together the way I wanted us to be.

I slammed my math book shut. I still had my own dreams, even if things had changed.

It was time to finish Mom's present. Not that she deserved one this year, but her birthday was next week and I figured it couldn't hurt to remind her she once had a family. A real one, with two kids, a mom, *and* a dad.

CHAPTER NINETEEN

There are quite a few cars parked out on the street," Mom said as she pulled up in front of Lydia's house the next night. "Are you sure your OM team is meeting again tonight? I thought you were meeting this weekend."

"We had to add an extra day since we have so much work to do," I said as I got out of the car. "I'll call you when it's over."

"Okay. See you later. Love you!"

I didn't say it back. You couldn't tell your daughter that you'd been lying to her for years and expect things to go back the way they were before. Mom wanted to act like everything was perfectly normal. Well, too bad for her.

I stood on the curb and watched as Mom drove off. If she could have secrets, then I could, too.

"Sunny?" Lydia's eyes were wide when she saw me at the front door. "What are you doing here?"

"I saw the flyer about the animal rights meeting. I hope it's okay."

Lydia stared at me. "*You* want to join our animal rights protest? Where'd you see the flyer?"

"First at your store, then in the basement—"

"You were snooping around?"

I shook my head, then looked down at the floor. Maybe this was a stupid idea, just like all my stupid ideas to get my parents back together. A protest wasn't going to change my grandmother's mind about her fur store, and coming to the meeting wasn't going to change Lydia's mind about me. "I—I thought it was open to anyone. I can call my mom, if you want."

Lydia shook her head and grabbed me by the wrist. "Come on!" she said as she led me downstairs. "Now I won't be the only kid here."

It wasn't the warmest welcome I'd ever been given, but I took it. In the basement, around ten people stood talking and eating the snacks that Lydia's mom had laid out on the coffee table. "Hey, everyone," Lydia said. "This is Sunny."

All the grown-ups turned and stared at me. If it were up to me, I'd have dropped right through the middle of the floor. But the grown-ups seemed friendly enough; most of them smiled or waved. Lydia handed me a name tag and a cup of cider. I was helping myself to some vegetables and dip when Mrs. Applebaum asked everyone to sit down so we could start the meeting.

"Welcome to the Bennetsville chapter of the North Carolina Network for Animals. It's so good to see all of you!" She looked around at everyone, then turned to her chart paper. "Let's begin by brainstorming all of the issues you're particularly interested in tackling this year. Next, we'll focus on our plans for Fur-Free Friday, which takes place at the end of next month."

My ears wiggled when she said Fur-Free Friday. *Hurry up and talk about the protest already!* It was all I could think about while Lydia's mom wrote things down on the board.

After she filled up the chart, she said, "As you can see, we have a lot to work on. That means we need to focus on recruiting new members."

I sighed louder than I'd meant to. During the boring discussion about membership, I got up to refill my snack plate. By the time I sat back down, Mrs. Applebaum had finally gotten around to what I'd been waiting for: Fur-Free Friday.

"We'll meet at noon on Carson Boulevard, the side near Luxury Furs and Leathers."

My heart took a leap.

"If you've never been in a protest before, remember to keep walking back and forth. Also, you can't step foot on the sidewalk in front of the store. That's private property."

"How will the owner see us if we're out on the main street instead of on the mall sidewalk?" someone asked.

"Oh, she'll see us, all right," Mrs. Applebaum said. "More importantly, customers will see us as they turn off the main road into the shopping center."

Everyone started talking about what would happen at the protest, and the rest of the meeting was spent organizing committees to get the word out. Mrs. Applebaum said she'd contact the police and write up the press releases. "A sizable crowd would make our statement a lot stronger. Tell all your friends, and we need to post notices now to let people know about this protest."

I called Mom as soon as the meeting was over. I took the phone upstairs to the kitchen so she wouldn't hear all the noise. Those animal rights people sure liked to talk and talk. The meeting had lasted longer than I expected, and I was afraid she was going to get suspicious.

"I'm already in the driveway," Mom said. "I was about to come to the door and get you."

"I'll be right out," I told her, handing the phone to Lydia, who had followed me up the steps.

"Are you really going to come to the protest?"

I shrugged. "I don't think Mom will let me."

"Hey, I've got an idea! You can be the one to dress up in the animal costume. No one will ever know it's you."

"I don't know," I said, but the wheels in my mind were already turning. "I mean, I just came to the meeting to see what it was all about."

"You should do it, Sunny. If you really want to speak up for the animals."

"I'll think about it," I said as I opened the front door.

"I'm glad you came to the meeting," Lydia said.

I turned to her and smiled. "Me, too."

Mom honked the horn and I raced outside. "It's almost nine o'clock," she said as soon I got in the car. "Pretty late for a meeting on a school night, don't you think?"

I shrugged. "We were in the middle of something so Coach Baker let us keep working."

Mom gave me a good, hard look. "Sunny, are you telling me the truth?"

"Of course," I said. Mom had lied to me, so I could lie right back. But I couldn't shut off the little voice in the back of my head saying, *Another lie? What's wrong with you? First you lied to Jessie about the OM meeting. You're not telling Lydia the truth about your grandmother . . . and now you're sneaking out*

to go to an animal rights meeting without telling your mom. You
better, fess up before it's too late. . . .

"I didn't see any other kids being picked up."

"I'm the last one," I said, trying to shut off that voice in
my head. Just then a couple of people came out of the house,
talking and laughing. And they weren't kids.

"So who are *they*? And why are all these cars parked in
front of the house?"

"I don't know. We were downstairs working. Maybe
Lydia's mom had some friends over or something."

Mom raised her eyebrows at me, like she wasn't going
for it. I put on the playlist I'd made for her and turned up the
volume. That's when Mom's phone rang.

"Jeb? Hi!" Her voice went up two or three octaves as a
man's voice came over the speakers. She didn't seem to notice
that she'd turned off Scott's "Songs of Love" playlist, just so
she could talk to some strange guy.

Not that any of that mattered anymore.

I listened in on the conversation, but even though Mom
sounded excited to be talking to Jeb, it was all about pacing
and character arcs and soon I tuned her out.

The only good thing about the phone call was that Mom
was so busy, I was able to jump out and run inside while she
was still talking about plot.

***

I could tell Scott felt bad about what had happened as soon as I picked up the phone on Friday evening. It was our regular night to talk, so I figured I'd frozen him out long enough.

Scott's voice was soft and a little uncertain, like he wasn't sure what to say even though I knew he'd been thinking about it for days. He waited for me to speak, and when I didn't, he cleared his throat. "I'm really sorry, Sunny. I don't know how that photo got in there. I didn't want you to find out this way."

"Mom said the same thing."

"I know, honey. We should have told you the truth sooner—"

"So why didn't you?"

Scott paused. "I guess—well, it's something that happened in the past. Just because Mark was there when you were born doesn't change the fact that we've been together as a family since you were a little girl."

"*Pretending* to be a family," I corrected him. "Just like you and Mom were *pretending* to be boyfriend and girlfriend."

"Now, hold on a second. We've never pretended anything. Maybe our family is different from others—"

"Way different. Abnormally different. We never even lived in the same house, and now we're not even living in the same state!"

"Having separate homes didn't seem to matter. Before you moved to North Carolina, we spent a lot of time together—"

"Well, we're not spending much time together now."

"Your mom needed a change—"

"You guys keep saying that, but you're just making excuses! You told us we were moving because Mom wanted to go back to school when that was only *part* of the story. And telling *part* of the story is the same as a lie, so you lied to us more than once. Multiple times." I let out a big breath, right into the phone.

Scott's voice got quiet. "I can't tell you how sorry I am that we didn't have an honest talk with you before the move. Everything just seemed to be happening so fast. We were so busy working out details about what was going to happen next that we didn't stop to think about what was happening to you and Autumn, the people we cared more about than anyone else in the world."

"You didn't try to stop her. If you really cared that much about us, you wouldn't have let us go."

"Oh, Sunflower. You know when your mom makes her mind up about something, there's no stopping her."

I thought about that for a minute, remembering how things between Mom and Scott had changed over the summer. They'd never argued in front of us, but being around them hadn't felt comfortable, the way it always had. It was like there was a string stretching between them, and it was pulled so tight it could have snapped at any second. I thought it was because they were breaking up, but maybe it was really because Scott was afraid of losing us. "You didn't want us to go, did you?" I asked.

"Of course not. But I couldn't get in the way of your mom's dreams."

What about my dreams? My dreams for us to be one big family in a place that was already home? Why did my dreams—and Autumn's, too—count for less than Mom's?

"Look, the most important thing is that I love you. I love you and Autumn as much as any dad could love his daughters."

I shrugged. Tears stung my eyes. *What about you and Mom?* I wanted to ask. But the pieces of the jigsaw puzzle were beginning to fit into place. I'd suspected it since Mom told me about the photo, but talking to Scott made it more clear. He was the one who had stepped in after Mark died. He's the one who had always put Mom first. And now that I thought of it, Mom had never looked at Scott the same way he looked at her. Mom had been in love with Mark, and Scott had tried to help, but he couldn't take Mark's place. Maybe that's why he never talked about his twin brother.

Love was way more complicated than it seemed in Disney movies.

"After Mark died," Scott continued, "we decided we were going to stay together, to help each other out and to be there for you, no matter what."

"What about now?" I asked. "Mom won't tell me what's going to happen when she finishes her degree, and now that things are different—"

"The only thing that's different is that you know more about the situation than you did a week ago. Two years is a long way off. In the meantime, I'll be there at Christmas, and you can spend a few weeks with me next summer . . ." I stopped listening as Scott started listing all the fun things we'd do when we got together. Two words echoed in my head: *two years.*

Two years *was* a long way off. In two years, I'd be almost fourteen. Practically grown up. My mind reeled thinking of everything that could happen.

Mom could start dating Jeb (ugh) or some other guy from her writing classes, or even worse, some "old flame." She could get offered a job at a college in North Carolina, or somewhere across the country, and we'd move even farther away.

Scott could meet someone else who was going back to college like he was, or he could start dating a customer at the bookstore. Scott could end up with someone with kids. Presto! Bingo! He'd have a totally new family.

And where did all that leave me? Scott had never adopted me, and since Mom and Scott weren't married, there'd be no custody agreement like there was with my friend Madeline when her parents got divorced. No guaranteed visits. As Scott moved on with his new life there'd be fewer and fewer phone calls and emails, since he'd assume we were moving on with our new lives, too, in Nebraska or *Alaska* or wherever Mom decided to go.

A little more time would pass, and then *poof!* I'd disappear from Scott's thoughts completely, leaving only a shadow behind.

Just like a photo in an album.

There was only one way to guarantee I wouldn't disappear from my dad's life: I had to find a way to make Mom move us back to New Jersey where he couldn't forget about me.

And I wasn't waiting two years to do it.

CHAPTER TWENTY

From: MadelineL@ilovebooks.com
To: SunnyKid@CreativityisCool.com
Witches and Goblins and Ghosts, Oh My!

What are you going to be for Halloween this year? I'm
dressing up as a witch again. My hat still fits, but my dress
is getting a little tight and way too short. Mom says it's
the last year I can wear it because it's totally inappropriate.
Hahahaha!

Miss you,
Maddy

P.S. Stellaluna is doing great.

From: SunnyKid@CreativityisCool.com
To: MadelineL@ilovebooks.com
Re: Witches and Goblins and Ghosts, Oh My!

I'm dressing up as a witch, too.

Miss you,
Sunny

From: Scott@BookBuyers.com
To: SunnyKid@CreativityisCool.com

Thanks for the photo, Sunny! Your mom must have had fun signing up for Glamour Shots.

You know what I'd really like? A photo of you and Autumn outside your new house. I could hang it up at work so I could look at your faces whenever I want to.

Love,
Scott

***

"So, what did your dad say about the photo?" Jessie asked me in art class. "I bet he can't stop looking at her, right?"

I shrugged. As much as I liked Jessie, I wasn't about to try to explain everything to her. Like Mom said, it was complicated.

"Well? Did you send it to him?"

"Sure," I said. I'd told Mom I needed to send something to Madeline, and she'd taken me to the post office the Monday after we did the makeover. By the time Scott received it, though, everything had already fallen apart. "He didn't have much to say about it."

"Oh." Jessie put down her pencil and looked up at me. "Maybe he's just keeping it to himself right now."

"Maybe. Thanks for doing the makeover, anyway."

Jessie squeezed my wrist. "Your mom's really pretty. I bet he'll come around," she said, but her voice didn't sound as confident as it usually did. She'd seen with her own parents that there wasn't much kids could do when it came to making their parents fall in love.

We worked in silence for a while, drawing pieces of popcorn Ms. Rusgo had placed on red cloth at the front of the room.

"You want to come over on Wednesday?" Jessie asked a few minutes later. "We can do something besides makeovers."

"Wednesday? I have Odyssey of the Mind practice after school. How about Thursday?"

Jessie shook her head. "Can't. Tomorrow I have dance, and cheerleading tryouts are Thursday and Friday."

"Maybe another time, then?" I said.

"Maybe," Jessie replied. "But I might be pretty busy from now on. Everyone thinks I'm going to make the team, and we have practice every day after school!"

***

Grandma Grace was frosting a three-layer cake when we got home after the OM meeting on Wednesday. "Mmm, something smells good," I said, taking in a big whiff of sugary air.

"Is it my favorite?" Mom stuck a finger in the frosting. "Hummingbird cake?"

"Of course," Grandma Grace said with a smile. "Did you think I'd forget?"

After dinner I had my first taste of hummingbird cake, which was full of stuff like pineapple, bananas, and cinnamon, topped with cream cheese frosting. I liked chocolate better, but Mom took a bite and said, "Oh, this is heavenly."

When it was time to open presents, I held on to mine even though it didn't matter anymore. "Open it last," I said, so Mom tore into the other gifts: some pottery Autumn had made in school, a book called *How to Write the Breakout Novel* from Scott, and a leather purse from Grandma Grace.

"Of course I know you'll never wear a fur coat," Grandma Grace said to my mom, "but I thought you might like this purse. It's a designer bag, from Italy."

"Thanks, Mom. I've never had anything quite so . . . expensive-looking." She ran her fingers across it.

"It won't fall apart after a couple of months, like your other handbags," Grandma Grace said. She was probably right about that. Mom liked to carry these bags made of velvet or cloth. When the straps fell off she'd safety pin them together until the zippers broke, and then it was time to get a new purse.

"Hey, did you get anything from your secret admirer?" Autumn asked. "I bet he remembered it was your birthday."

Mom shook her head. "Nope, not a thing. Not even a flower on the doorstep."

I bit my lip and looked down at the gift-wrapped photo album in my lap. Would they ever guess the flowers were from me?

"Oh, look!" Mom picked up a card from the table, and I was relieved she'd changed the subject. The last thing I felt like talking about was her secret admirer. "It's from Scott." When she opened it up, his voice surrounded us.

"Hey, it's one of those singing cards!" Autumn said. "How'd he do that?"

"Let me see," I said, reaching for the card.

"He recorded his own voice," Mom said as Scott sang a James Taylor tune and played guitar. I watched Mom and, for a moment, I thought I caught a faraway look in her eyes. But it flickered away, and the next thing I knew she was reaching for my present.

She tore off the wrapping paper and stared down at the cover, where I'd written: *Our Lives by Sunny Beringer.* Mom looked up at me. "You put together a photo album for my birthday?"

I nodded. "All our photos are on the computer. We didn't even bring any of the old albums with us."

"Oh, I love it!" Mom said, flipping through the pages.

"I thought you were printing the pictures for a school project," Autumn said.

"It was supposed to be a surprise."

"Well, it certainly is," Mom said, and I could see she was still trying to figure it all out.

"There are some really old ones in there," I told her. "Scott sent me a bunch of pictures."

Mom's eyes caught mine for a second, and I knew she was thinking about the one in the hospital. I watched as she flipped back through the pages. "It's been years since I've seen some of these pictures," she said when she got to the end. "What made you decide to tackle a project like this one?"

I shrugged and looked down at the giftwrap scattered across the table. "Just wanted to, I guess."

"Well, it's really nice to have a family album." Mom squeezed my hand. "I will always treasure it."

"Scott will love it, too," Autumn said, and then she opened his card again. "And listen!" She giggled. "Now it's like he's right here celebrating with us."

I listened as his voice filled the room, making me feel empty inside. I'd worked on my special gift for weeks and it didn't matter anymore. Scott was singing "You've Got a Friend" to Mom from miles away, and Mom seemed perfectly happy about the situation.

CHAPTER TWENTY-ONE

From: MadelineL@ilovebooks.com
To: SunnyKid@CreativityisCool.com
Snowstorm!

It started snowing on Halloween, but we went trick-or-treating anyway! This year I took a pillowcase instead of my pumpkin bag, and I filled it all the way up to the top!

Here's a picture of me and Emma dressed as witches.

Hope you had fun, too!

***

I should have written back to Madeline right away. Instead, I hit DELETE without responding. It was the first year I'd gone trick-or-treating without her. From the picture she'd sent, it didn't seem like she'd noticed. I tagged along with Autumn and her new friend, Hallie. Nothing had felt right about the evening except that I ended up with a bag full of candy.

Jessie had gone trick-or-treating with Chloe, Meghan, and Cassie. They talked about it at lunch, right in front of me. Jessie wasn't being mean or anything. She just didn't think about including me since she'd already made plans with her other friends. After all, they'd been trick-or-treating together for years.

Besides, she probably guessed that I didn't feel that comfortable hanging out with the other girls. She knew I didn't fit in with her crowd, and wouldn't fit in with her new cheerleading friends either, now that she'd made the team.

I let that miserable "I don't fit in anywhere" feeling settle over me for a few minutes. By the time it made its way to the pit of my stomach, I'd pulled out the notebook that once had held "Sunny's Super-Stupendous Plan to Get Mom and Dad Back Together" and turned to a clean page.

It was time to come up with a new plan.

I tapped my pen against the paper. Nothing. I starting drawing: pictures of Stellaluna, the tire swing in the backyard, the front of Book Buyers with its striped green and white awnings. Still nothing.

Not a single creative thought had popped into my mind.

Glancing out the window, I spotted Ripple in the corner of the yard. I dropped my pen and headed outside, looking for inspiration. Or, at least, a break from thinking.

Ripple came right out from the bushes. I ran my hands over her as she rubbed against me. She pushed her head under my hand so I wouldn't stop petting her. As much as I liked Ripple, taking care of a stray cat would never take the place of Stellaluna, who used to jump up on my lap when I came home from school every day, and who slept curled up beside me on my bed every night.

I closed my eyes and imagined I was petting Stellaluna's soft fur . . .

Soft fur, like the fur on the coats hanging up in Grandma Grace's store.

Eureka! That was *it*! I jumped up, pumping my arms in the air. The solution to my problems had been right there, staring me in the face the whole time. Thanks to Lydia and her fur protest, the perfect opportunity to get back home was waiting for me. And I could finally speak up for the animals at the same time.

You'll have to lie some more and do some more sneaking around, that little voice started whispering again. *And what about your grandmother?*

I shut my eyes tight, blocking out the voice. Somehow, it would all work out. People would understand that I didn't have a choice. It was going to take courage to make this plan work, and I couldn't let anything get in my way.

After I fed Ripple, I ran back up the steps to my room and pulled out my notebook. It was time to get started on "Sunny's Super-Stupendous Plan . . . to Get Back Home."

***

"Listen carefully," Coach Baker said at the OM meeting later that week. "'Unlike Shakespeare's Hamlet, the team's character will take the easy way out, only to discover it was the wrong choice. Teams will incorporate a character to portray Hamlet's conscience, a creative scene change, and the use of a trapdoor.'" Coach Baker looked up at us. "What's your main character's dilemma?"

"Annalise Alien flunked her telekinesis test because she didn't practice," Lydia said. "She doesn't want to get into the School for Paranormal Education. She wants to be a pastry chef."

"She was too busy baking chocolate moon pies instead of studying," I said.

"Okay," Coach Baker said, pacing in front of us. "And how did Annalise take the easy way out?"

"She didn't want to tell her mother the truth, so she ran away from home," Jamie, an eighth-grade boy, said.

"That's when she falls through the trapdoor," Carson explained.

"Good! How does the easy way out turn out to be the wrong choice?"

"She gets whisked to Earth, and ends up in the middle of a spooky dark forest," Jalia said.

"Battling ghosts," Avi added.

"Ooo!" Some of the kids made ghost sounds.

"Excellent," Coach Baker said. "It would have been better for her to face her mother and be true to herself. Instead, she took the easy way out. All right, so how do you plan to build the trapdoor and incorporate a creative scene change?"

Everyone started talking at once about how Annalise Alien would get whisked to Earth, but I tuned them out while the words *easy way out* echoed in my head. If I used the fur protest to let my grandmother know how I felt about her store and to get back home, I wasn't confronting my problems head on. It sure seemed I was a lot like Annalise Alien, running away from the truth.

Lydia nudged me. "Come on," she said as she grabbed her notebook. She motioned me to a table in the back where Jalia was already seated. "Coach Baker said to start drawing sketches."

"Okay, sure." Something had shifted between Lydia and me in the last few weeks, and it felt good to be included. As I picked up my notebook to follow her, I tried to push away all thoughts about choices that could lead me to battle my own ghosts, just like Annalise.

***

On the Monday before Thanksgiving break, I turned to Jessie in art class. "I'm not going to be able to sit with you at lunch today," I told her. "I hope that's okay, but there's someone I need to talk to."

Jessie squinted at me. "Who?"

"Oh, just someone from English class." I wasn't trying to keep my friendship with Lydia a secret, but I knew how Jessie felt about her.

Jessie shrugged. "Catch you tomorrow then," she said as she headed out of the classroom. I watched her walk down the hall, shoulders squared and head held high, as if she hadn't even given me a second thought. Didn't it matter to her at all if I sat with her at lunch? Would she miss me if I sat somewhere else every day?

I picked up my backpack from the art table and started toward the cafeteria, trying not to think about Jessie. I had important details of a plan to work out, and worrying about who liked me in Bennetsville was not on my list of things to do.

Catching a glimpse of red, curly hair at the back of the cafeteria, I found Lydia sitting at a table with Jalia from OM, Sierra from history class, and a couple of other girls I didn't know.

"Hi," I said, walking up to the table. For a moment, I hesitated. What if Lydia said I couldn't sit with them just to get back at me for what I did to her at the beginning of the year? I took a deep breath. "Mind if I sit here?"

Lydia looked around at the rest of the girls. "If it's okay with everyone else . . ."

The others nodded and Jalia said, "Sure, Sunny. The more the merrier."

"Thanks," I said, trying to hide my relief as I put my lunch box down and pulled up a chair next to Lydia.

We talked about OM for a while before Lydia said, "Have you decided about the protest? It's next Friday, you know."

I nodded, and my heart rate sped up. "Actually, that's what I wanted to talk to you about. I think I can come . . . as long as I can wear the costume."

Lydia's eyes opened wide and she grabbed my arm. "You'll be perfect! I'll have to ask Mom, but I'm sure she'll say it's okay."

"Really?" So far, things were turning out easier than I had expected.

"Really." Lydia turned to the rest of the table. "Ladies, meet our official bunny for Fur-Free Friday!" The other girls clapped, and I felt my cheeks flush with pride. Lydia turned back to me. "No one else is brave enough to join us at the protest—"

"I told you Lydia, we're going out of town, or else I'd be there," Jalia said.

Some of the other girls echoed Jalia's words, though I wondered if they meant it. Being around Lydia could make you feel guilty for not doing more to help.

"Is someone coming out from the newspaper to take pictures?" I asked.

"Yup. All three TV stations are coming, too."

"Do you think they'd take pictures . . . of me? Since not that many kids protest?"

"I'm sure they will. I've been on TV tons of times. Maybe they'll even interview you."

I tried to keep from jumping up and down. "I'll talk to them," I said, my voice as matter-of-fact as I could manage.

"This is going to be great," Lydia said. "I'll tell Mom and she'll set something up. She'll be so excited to hear you're joining the protest!"

CHAPTER TWENTY-TWO

From: MadelineL@ilovebooks.com
To: SunnyKid@CreativityisCool.com
Happy Turkey Day!

Did you get my last email? I sent you a picture of me dressed up for Halloween. I missed you this year. We could have been three witches instead of two! Plus, Emma wouldn't trade any of her candy—not even the ones with coconut!

I've scanned a special Thanksgiving card I made for you. I can't draw like you, but it's supposed to be a turkey. I would have mailed it, but thought this would be quicker. Hope you have a happy Thanksgiving!

Love,
Maddy

P.S. Write back soon.

***

Thanksgiving was one of my favorite holidays. Usually, Scott would bring in an extra table and we'd set it up in the living room for all the guests: Aunt Louisa and Uncle Alan; my cousins, Ellie and Max; the Bumgardners, the old neighbors who lived across the street; and always one or two people from Book Buyers who didn't have anywhere to go for the holiday.

Mom and Scott would cook all day and the house would fill up with delicious smells. They'd turn on the stereo and sing along while Autumn and I watched the Thanksgiving Parade on TV. It was the one day when kids weren't allowed in the kitchen until it was time to eat.

Finally, everyone would arrive and we'd sit down for dinner and watch from the living room window as the sun began to set behind the mostly bare trees. Our small living room would fill up with voices and laughter. After dessert, we'd hang out with our cousins until it got late, then Mom would pull out the sleeping bags and let us watch a movie in her bedroom until the grown-ups decided it was time to go home.

This year, everything was different. Scott had already told us he'd rather come for a longer visit over Christmas, which of course was a sign of things to come. First Scott makes an excuse why he can't be with us for Thanksgiving, next he'll say he can't make a trip for our birthdays, and before you know it . . . we're down to one visit each year. Maybe none.

Grandma Grace planned Thanksgiving dinner for 5:00 p.m. and she put us to work.

"Make sure you polish until it shines." She handed Autumn and me her good silver, a tub of polish, and a rag. "Be careful not to leave any streaks."

Autumn glanced over at me. I knew what she was thinking: *Why are we using the good silver anyway, when it's just us for dinner?* Grandma Grace had already told us that she was skipping her usual visit to Raleigh with her sister, Great Aunt Elizabeth, so she could have Thanksgiving at home with her grandchildren this year.

I wish she had gone to Raleigh. I would have had more fun sleeping late and eating macaroni and cheese from a box than going through all this fuss. The only good thing about cooking turkey was that Ripple would get a lot of delicious leftovers.

After we finished polishing, it was time to set the table with Grandma Grace's extra special china. Then came the crystal goblets.

"Be careful," Grandma Grace warned when I clanked two together before setting them down next to the plates.

After the table looked like something out of her favorite magazine, *Southern Living*, she put us to work washing and drying dishes, and sweeping the floor while the Macy's parade played on TV in the living room, unwatched.

I didn't want to think about how everything felt so wrong on Thanksgiving, so I focused on my plan for Fur-Free Friday instead. So far, I'd dodged all the potholes: Mom wasn't suspicious because I had convinced her I'd gone to an OM meeting. Lydia hadn't asked any questions about why I had to wear the suit. Grandma Grace wouldn't see me outside protesting because I'd be dressed like a bunny.

I had written out a plan in my notebook:

1. Convince Mom we have to go shopping for winter clothes on Friday after lunch.

2. Wake up Friday morning with a terrible stomachache, but feel better by noon so you can convince Mom to still go shopping and pick up a little something for you.

3. As soon as Mom and Autumn leave, ride your bike to Evergreen Plaza.

4. Meet Lydia at Earthly Goods and change into your costume.

5. Make sure the newspaper reporter spells your name correctly.

6. Make sure the reporter knows you're the grand-daughter of the fur store owner.

Dinner was served promptly at five. When Autumn and I got up to help with the serving plates, Grandma Grace shooed us out of the kitchen. "You've done enough to help, girls," she told us. "Go ahead and have a seat."

We waited while Mom and Grandma Grace placed one dish after another on hot plates in the middle of the long table. Familiar dishes. Dishes that we'd had every year for Thanksgiving and loved. Mom's famous sweet potato casserole with sticky walnuts on top. Scott's French green beans with salted almonds. Aunt Louisa's stuffing. Uncle Alan's mashed potatoes, the kind with cheddar cheese swirled in. Mom's pineapple casserole with cornflakes on top. Thick pieces of corn bread, the kind you make in a skillet.

"You made all of our favorite things!" Autumn said. "Just like at home!"

"It was your grandmother's idea," Mom said, looking over at Grandma Grace.

"I know how much you girls miss being home for Thanksgiving," Grandma Grace said. She cleared her throat. "It's a real treat to celebrate with all of you this year, so I wanted to do something special."

Mom reached over and squeezed Grandma Grace's hand. Maybe I was seeing things since the room was dim, lit only by candles. But for a minute, it looked like my grandmother's eyes were shiny with tears.

My grandmother had done all of this . . . for us.

A pain shot through my side, and tears filled my eyes. For a moment, I wondered if maybe I really was going to be sick for Fur-Free Friday. But the pain went away as quickly as it had come, taking my appetite with it.

If all went according to my plan, tomorrow I would stand in front of the TV cameras and say hurtful things to my grandmother.

"So what are we waiting for?" Autumn asked, breaking the silence. "Let's eat!"

***

The day after Thanksgiving, sunlight poured through my window, waking me. I sat up and rubbed my eyes, glancing at my alarm clock. Eleven minutes after seven. I pulled the covers back over my head and rolled over. But it didn't take long to figure out that it's impossible to sleep when your mind is wide awake.

I turned my plan over and over in my mind, thinking of everything that could go wrong.

It would work perfectly, as long as Mom didn't cancel her shopping trip or cut it short. But what if Grandma Grace spotted me in the parking lot before I changed into the costume? And what if the reporters didn't want to interview a kid? I'd have to chase them down and beg them to print my photo and my full name, including that important little detail about who I was related to.

I counted a million ways the whole thing could fall apart.

One thing I wouldn't let myself think about was what my grandmother would think of me when she saw me in the paper, or hopefully, on the news. If I worried about that, I knew I'd back out. And then where would I be?

Stuck in Bennetsville without a dad, that's where.

I got up and slipped on jeans and a heavy sweater. I touched my hand against the window. Another cold November day, but the sky was clear and blue. The fur protest wouldn't be cancelled because of rain.

My heart sped up as I thought about the next few hours. If my plan worked, we could be back in New Jersey with Scott and Stellaluna and Madeline . . . by next weekend.

And if it failed? I pushed the thought right out of my mind.

CHAPTER TWENTY-THREE

Grandma Grace left for the store early, "to keep an eye on those animal rights nutcases." By the time I made it downstairs for breakfast, I didn't have to fake a stomachache. Real pain was gnawing away at the pit of my stomach.

I sat down at the table and dropped my head onto my arms. "No pumpkin bread for me," I said, even though Grandma Grace's was the best on the planet.

"Sunny, what's wrong?" Mom asked.

I moaned.

"What is it—your head?" Mom put her hand on my forehead.

I moaned again and clutched my stomach.

"Hmm . . . it doesn't feel like you have a fever." Mom touched my hands. "As a matter of fact, you're ice-cold."

"Maybe you ate too much Thanksgiving dinner," Autumn said.

"I think I have a stomach virus," I said in a weak voice.

"Actually," Mom said, "you did leave a lot of food on your plate last night. Guess you're coming down with something. Let's hope it's the twenty-four-hour version. All right, off to bed. I'll be up with some tea and toast."

"Ohhh," I said dramatically as I stood up, half bent-over, and walked slowly to the steps. I had to make this good. "Ohhh," I groaned again as I made my way upstairs.

"What about me?" Autumn asked. "We're still going shopping, aren't we?"

"Sorry, hon. We'll have to miss the sales. Your sister's sick."

"Aww," Autumn said. "I need some winter clothes!"

I stopped groaning and turned around quickly. "That's okay. I'll be fine at home by myself."

"I don't think that's a good idea," Mom said. "The shopping can wait."

"No, I mean it. Besides, I need you to pick up some sweaters for me."

"See?" Autumn said. "Sunny will be fine, right?"

"Right," I said. "You should go."

Mom looked over at me. "I'm not making any decisions right now. Go on upstairs and we'll see how you're feeling after a while."

I got undressed and climbed back into bed. Since the protest wasn't until two, I'd have plenty of time to feel a little better . . . but not feel well enough to go shopping.

A few hours later, with Autumn's help, I somehow convinced Mom that I'd be all right on my own. When they left the house a little after one, I watched from my window until the car pulled out of the driveway. Then I jumped out of bed and started racing around the room as fast as I could.

I pulled on jeans and my sweater, brushed my teeth, and ran my fingers through my hair. Not that it mattered what I looked like, since I'd be completely covered up anyway.

My stomach churned from hunger and nerves. This had to work. It just had to!

Sweat trickled down my back even though it was a cool November day as I rode my bike toward the shopping center. By the time I saw the parking lot up ahead, people were already gathering on the sidewalk. I turned into the strip mall on the side farthest from Luxury Furs. After locking my bike in the rack, I ran over to Earthly Goods where Lydia was waiting for me.

"Sorry I'm late," I said, trying to catch my breath.

"Oh, it's no problem." Lydia grabbed the costume bag out of the backseat of their car. "I'm so glad you came! You can change right here, if you want."

I glanced around and shook my head. We were still too close to Luxury Furs and Leathers to feel safe. "Can I use your bathroom?"

"Sure." Lydia pushed open the door and waved at a man with longish hair and glasses. "Hi, Dad! This is Sunny."

"Hi," I said.

"I've heard you're going to be our raccoon," he said with a smile.

"Raccoon?" I asked. "I thought I was going to be a rabbit."

"We found someone else for the bunny costume," Lydia explained. "But you're small enough to be the raccoon."

I shrugged. "Okay," I said as I made my way to the bathroom. I stepped into the suit and zipped it up as quick as I could. Then I put on the raccoon head.

"You look great!" Lydia said when I came out. I could barely see her through the eye holes, and the suit was big and baggy. I wondered why Lydia had said they needed someone small for this costume.

"I hope I don't trip," I said, but my voice came out muffled and Lydia couldn't understand me.

"Just don't talk," she said. "Follow me. I'll tell you what to do."

I nodded, waved to Lydia's dad as he called out "Good luck!" and carefully made my way down the sidewalk and up the hill where the protest was already under way.

"Hi, Sunny!" Mrs. Applebaum greeted me as we walked up to the stack of signs on the grass. "Don't worry about holding a sign. I think you'll be more effective in that cage over there."

I looked over to where Mrs. Applebaum was pointing. A big wire cage sat on the ground with a sign beside it that said CAGED ANIMALS WAITING FOR DEATH.

"I have to get inside that cage?" I asked, but it came out more like "Mwa mwa mwa mwa mwamwa mwa mwa?"

"Sorry, honey," Mrs. Applebaum said, "I can't understand you with that mask on. Don't worry, you'll be fine. The protest won't last long."

Now I got why Lydia had said I was the right size for the raccoon. If we kept to the schedule, I'd have to spend the next ninety minutes inside the cage. As I climbed inside the cramped quarters in my bulky suit, ninety minutes sounded like a really long time.

But, as I looked out at the other protesters marching up and down the sidewalk with their signs, I realized this was my chance to be a real activist. I was finally speaking up for what I believed in, even if it meant I had to crouch down behind bars to do it.

I was glad to see we had a good crowd. The line stretched all the way across Carson Boulevard. A few minutes later police cars pulled into the parking lot in front of Luxury Furs with their blue lights flashing.

For a moment, I thought about my grandmother. Was she worried when she saw the lights? Maybe she was thinking about those fur coats hanging on the racks, seeing for the first time that a lot of animals had died horrible deaths to make them. If a bunch of people were willing to march outside her shop on a cold winter day, did it make her wonder if she was doing something wrong? Or did she still think we were just a bunch of animal rights fanatics who didn't know what we were talking about?

"How are you doing in there?" Lydia asked when she passed me.

I gave her a thumbs up, or rather a paw up, to show that I was fine. Well, maybe not fine, exactly. I finally understood why people get claustrophobia. But I'd stay in the cage all day if it would get the reporters' attention.

"Don't worry about the police," Lydia told me. "They're here to make sure there's not any trouble."

I wanted to ask Lydia if her mom had arranged the interview, but it was impossible to talk with the raccoon head on. So I just nodded again, crossing my fingers inside my costume as Lydia marched past. Channel Two, Channel Seven, and Channel Twenty-Eight interviewed Darlene for the six o'clock news. A newspaper reporter showed up, too, flashing his camera in my direction.

"Only ten more minutes of protesting," Lydia's mom announced to everyone after her interviews were done. Then she kneeled down next to me. "Guess what, Sunny? A reporter from Channel Seven is waiting to speak with you."

"With me?" My heart sped up. It was all working out, exactly like I'd planned!

Mrs. Applebaum nodded as she helped me out of the cage. "They wanted to talk to the animal in the cage, especially after I told them you were only in middle school. Right over there," she said, pointing to a white van with the words CHANNEL SEVEN NEWS on the side. "Are you nervous?"

I pulled off my animal head. "Um, yeah." I bit my lip. This was it. If I did a good job with the interview, everything could change.

"Well, just relax," Mrs. Applebaum said, squeezing my hand through the costume. "Take a few deep breaths. You'll do great!"

"Thanks," I said. Slowly, I walked toward the cameras. I felt like I was in one of those movie scenes where the hero walks off into the sunset triumphantly. But I couldn't hold on to the image for long. I could just as easily be the tragic hero walking to my doom.

"Sunny?" Lydia called from behind me.

I turned around and she ran over and threw her arms around me. "Good luck!"

"I'm so proud of you," Mrs. Applebaum called to me. "It takes a lot of courage to speak up for what you believe in."

"Thanks," I mumbled as I turned away from them both and continued toward where the TV reporters stood, waiting. I didn't think Mrs. Applebaum would call me courageous if she knew I'd lied to my mom and was about to speak out against my own grandmother. There was probably a better word to describe me. I'm sure it wasn't a good one.

The lump in my throat was about the size of a grapefruit now, making it hard to swallow. I had turned into one of those not-so-nice people who do whatever it takes to get what they want.

As I neared the van, I saw a pretty lady with shiny, dark hair talking on her phone. She slipped the phone into the pocket of her jacket when she spotted me, thrusting out a hand to shake my raccoon paw. "Janine Turner," she said with a smile. "And you must be Sunny Beringer, the young lady I'll be interviewing today."

"Hi," I managed to say. "I've never been on TV before, so I might really botch this."

Janine laughed. "There's nothing to be nervous about. You know, this will be a wonderful human interest story. Grown-ups are always protesting one thing or another. But to find a child willing to stand up for something she believes in . . . well, that's something quite special. People will be curious to hear what you have to say."

Right now, the only person who needed to hear me was my grandmother, but I didn't tell Janine Turner that. I just nodded.

"Okay. Let me jot down a few details," she said, pulling out a notepad.

"How old are you, Sunny?"

"Eleven. I'll be twelve next month."

"And what school do you go to?"

"Evergreen Middle School. I'm in sixth grade."

Janine dropped her notepad on the seat of the van. "Are you ready?"

I nodded. *Ready as I'll ever be.*

"Just act natural," she said with a smile, then turned to the camera crew. "Okay, roll 'em!" She looked straight ahead and turned on her smooth broadcaster voice. Bright camera lights blinded me, and I blinked.

"Today we have a sixth grader from Evergreen Middle School, Sunny Beringer, who came out as part of the Fur-Free Friday protest." Janine turned to me. "We don't see many eleven-year-olds joining protests, unless they're with their parents. You came all by yourself. What made you decide to take a stand against fur?"

"I love animals," I said. My voice shook a little, matching my wobbly knees.

"That's certainly a good reason. Why did you decide to dress up in costume?"

Now that was a tough one. I couldn't tell them I did it so I'd end up on TV, or that I had to sneak out of the house to make my plan work—

"You certainly got people thinking about the animals behind the furs," Janine jumped right in.

"Um, yeah," I said. "I wanted people to think about the animals. The fur coats belong on their backs, not on ours."

"A very creative idea," Janine said, nodding at me. "What would you like to tell all those folks out there who think it's a luxury to wear fur?"

"Think about the animals. We wouldn't like it if someone killed us for our skin, so we shouldn't kill animals for their fur. It's definitely *not* a luxury for them."

"If you could speak to the owner of Luxury Furs and Leathers, what would you say to her?"

I squared my shoulders and stared straight into the camera. "I'd tell the owner that what she's doing should be against the law. Anyone who owns a fur store and says they're only trying to make people happy is a *big liar*. The owners who sell the furs are just as bad as those people who trap the animals and murder them for money."

"Wow, that's certainly a strong statement from a young girl. One who's fully committed to helping protect animals. Thank you for talking with us today." Then Janine turned back to the cameras. "This is Janine Turner with Sunny Beringer, live from Evergreen Plaza shopping center in Bennetsville."

The cameraman turned his lights off. "Nice job," Janine said with a wink. "Are you sure this is your first time on TV?"

"Positive," I said.

"You're a real pro. Watch Channel Seven at six tonight."

"Okay," I said as she climbed into her WAXZ van. "You know the owner of Luxury Furs and Leathers?"

She looked back at me. "Yes?"

"She's my grandmother."

CHAPTER TWENTY-FOUR

"How are you feeling?" Mom asked as she dropped her bags on the coffee table later that afternoon. I'd changed quickly and raced home, arriving twelve minutes before she and Autumn had pulled into the driveway.

"I'm fine," I said, though I was pretty much the opposite.

"You look much better," Mom said. "You got dressed, and everything."

"Oh, yeah." I looked down at my jeans. I'd forgotten I had been in pajamas when they left.

"Have you eaten anything?"

"I'm not hungry." I tried to look a little green again, which wasn't difficult.

"Look what I got," Autumn said, not worried about me at all. She emptied her bags onto the floor.

After Autumn showed me her new sweaters, she sat on the sofa to watch TV with me for a while, then headed up to her room. I kept watching the large hands of the grandfather clock.

The front door opened at five-thirty and in walked Grandma Grace. I couldn't even look at her. The empty feeling in my stomach turned into an ache. It was like how I felt after I'd walked away from Lydia at the lunch table, except about a hundred times worse.

"Guess what?" Grandma Grace said, dropping into her favorite recliner. "I'm going to be on the six o'clock news tonight."

Mom looked up from her laptop. "They interviewed you?"

"Sure did," Grandma Grace said. "I'm going to be a celebrity."

"Um, what channel?" I asked.

"Channel Two. WCNC."

I sucked in my breath. If Grandma Grace was being interviewed on Channel Two, we might miss my interview on Channel Seven! "Are you sure it's not Channel Seven? They always cover important stories."

"I wish they'd all interviewed me, but Channel Two was the only one."

There was only one solution. I'd have to control the remote. I reached for it and hid it behind the sofa cushions.

"Autumn! Come on down!" Mom called a few minutes later. "It's time for Grandma Grace's debut!"

"Now where's that remote?" Grandma Grace said.

"Here it is!" I pulled it from behind the sofa cushion, took a deep breath and flipped to Channel Seven.

Mom gave me a funny look. "Channel Two, remember?"

"Here, I'll take that," said Grandma Grace.

Now, what? I could only hope that all the stations weren't covering the story at the same time. Or that someone else would see me on TV and tell my grandmother about it. I'd come this far—my plan couldn't fail because of a remote, could it?

I chewed on my fingernails while we sat through the national news, unimportant stuff about deficits and budgets. Then the words "Fur-Free Friday" flashed on the screen and I bit my finger by mistake.

"Here it is!" Grandma Grace shouted. "Some fool even dressed up in an animal suit!"

"Shh, listen," Mom said.

Mrs. Applebaum was being interviewed. "We're out here today to let people know how cruel the fur industry is."

Grandma Grace shook her head and clicked her tongue. "That woman has caused nothing but trouble since she moved to Bennetsville. She should have stayed in California with all the other nutcases."

I had one leg crossed over the other, my foot tapping up against the coffee table. When Grandma Grace said "the other nutcases," my leg jerked into the air. Tea from Grandma Grace's glass spilled onto the table.

"Oops, sorry!" I watched as the tea soaked into the magazines. I got up from the sofa to get a towel. Grandma Grace didn't even notice.

"Look!" Mom said, moving her head to see around me. "It's Grandma Grace!"

I sank to the floor and turned to watch. I didn't hear the reporter's question because I was too busy thinking of what to do next. I had to get my hands on that remote as soon as she stopped talking, to at least catch the end of my interview on the other channel. If she heard the answer to the last question I'd been asked, it would be enough.

"Trappers keep wildlife populations in healthy balance," Grandma Grace was saying when I looked up at the TV. "Trapping is a good way to control rabies and other destructive problems caused by overpopulation. Animals were created to provide food and clothing for mankind."

"How about these people out here who don't think you should sell furs—the ones claiming cruelty to animals?" the reporter asked.

"I would say to them that they're lucky to live in a country where they can voice their opinions. We live in America, the land of freedom of speech and freedom of choice. It gives me the right to open my store and allow people the luxury of a beautiful fur coat for those who would like one."

"My grandma's going to be famous!" Autumn said when the interview was over. Grandma Grace beamed.

I didn't waste any time, lunging for the remote that now sat on the coffee table.

"Let's see what the other channels had to say."

I flipped to Channel Seven and heard a familiar voice. Mine.

"What in the world . . ." Grandma Grace sounded shocked as she leaned forward to hear better.

I stared straight ahead and practiced breathing. In, out. Inhale, exhale. I glanced up to see a big picture of myself dressed in the raccoon suit with the head in my hands. Hair was sticking up all over and I looked plain silly as I stared at the camera. At the bottom of the screen were the words "Sunflower Beringer, granddaughter of Grace Beringer, owner of Luxury Furs and Leathers."

"Sunny?" Mom sounded stunned.

"Well, I never," Grandma Grace muttered.

"Look, you're on TV!" Autumn said, practically falling off the sofa.

The remote slipped from my hand and fell to the floor.

None of us said a word during the interview. No one moved an inch either. I think my blood actually stopped flowing as I sat there watching myself on the screen.

When it was over, the announcer cut to a commercial. We all sat there without speaking—even Autumn—until Grandma Grace got up and snapped off the set. I waited for someone to start yelling.

"Well," Mom finally said. "I guess that explains the quick recovery."

Autumn's eyes opened wide. "You mean you weren't even sick? You pretended so you could protest against Grandma?"

I shrugged. I wanted to spout something about how Grandma Grace's shop deserved to be shut down, but my nerve had disappeared now that I was sitting in the same room with her.

"Sunny," my mom said, "I'm shocked. Totally shocked. I mean, I knew you were an animal lover, but to sneak out to a protest without telling me—"

"You never would have let me go."

"—and to go on TV the way you did—"

It was now or never. I summoned up my courage and looked right at my grandmother. "I had to do it. What Grandma Grace is doing is wrong. I'm ashamed to admit she's my grandmother."

The look on my grandmother's face made me turn away. Her shoulders sagged and her eyes filled with tears.

"Sunny Carson Beringer," my mom said, "I cannot believe the disrespect you've shown to your grandmother, after all she's done for us—"

I forced myself to say the next words: "She hasn't done anything for me. I never wanted to move into her fancy house to begin with. It's not like she actually cares about us or anything—"

"That. Is. Enough," Mom said, just as Grandma Grace got up from the sofa and reached for her purse. "Up to your room right now. I will deal with you later." She turned to my grandmother as I put on a show by stomping up to my room. I didn't rush though, slowing down enough on the stairs to hear what was going on.

"Where are you going?" she asked my grandmother.

"Out. I need to clear my head."

"I'm really sorry, Mom. I don't know what's gotten into her—"

"It's okay, Rebecca, really it is. At least I know her true feelings about me."

"This isn't like her at all."

Grandma Grace lowered her voice and so did Mom. I strained my ears but couldn't hear a thing until my grandmother left the house, shutting the door behind her.

I threw myself down on my pink flowered bedspread, feeling very little like the triumphant hero. I closed my eyes and all I could see was the hurt look on my grandmother's face.

CHAPTER TWENTY-FIVE

There was a knock on my door a few minutes later. I buried my face in my pillow, refusing to look at my mom as she pushed the door open and walked inside. The footsteps stopped right next to my bed. "All right, Sunny. Out with it."

When I didn't say anything, Mom nudged my shoulder. "Come on, Sunny. Sit up. I want answers, and I want them *now*."

I turned over. Mom stood in front of me with her arms crossed in front of her chest. "I am waiting for an explanation, and it better be a good one."

I gulped, trying to think up something, quickly. Explaining things to Mom was one part of the plan I hadn't thought through all the way. I'd figured Grandma Grace would kick us out immediately, and I could deal with Mom once we were on our way home. I knew she'd be angry at first, but she'd come around when it all worked out.

Getting from here to the happy ending seemed a lot further away than I'd counted on.

"Turning animals into fur coats is cruel," I told her, avoiding her eyes. "You know how I feel about Grandma Grace's fur store."

"Did it ever occur to you to talk to her about it? Did you really think you'd get her to change her mind by going on TV?"

I shrugged. "You told me not to say anything, remember? After all, she let us stay in her great big old house just so you could go back to school."

"So you thought talking to a reporter was a better solution? Did you ever, for a moment, stop and think about how it would make your grandmother feel?"

I shrugged again, feeling that same shooting pain in my side. What kind of a question was that? Didn't Mom know that I *couldn't* think about my grandmother's feelings? As strongly as I felt about the fur issue, it would have put an end to the plan—*snap!* Just like that. "It's not like it matters. She doesn't care about me anyway," I said, but even though the words came out of my own mouth, I no longer believed them.

"Now that," Mom said, her voice softer as she dropped to the bed next to me, "is totally untrue."

I couldn't say a thing. Mom was silent as if we were both trying to figure out what to do next.

"You know, Sunny," she finally said, "I really didn't know how things were going to work out when we moved in here. I knew you girls didn't have much of a relationship with your grandmother, and she'd always been so distant before."

"See? That's what I mean. Mostly we've been an inconvenience. Forgetting to take our shoes off, leaving our stuff around, and she has to cook for four now instead of one," I said in a weak attempt to convince myself and my mom.

Mom wasn't falling for it. "That's where you're wrong. Your grandmother has changed. She may like a neat house, but I've watched the way she takes an interest in both of you, the way she genuinely wants to know what's going on in your lives. And she's been trying to cook your favorite foods, and buy little things for you, and spend time with you."

I turned my back on Mom, not wanting her to see me crying.

"What I don't get is what you thought you'd accomplish with all this. Did you really think you'd change your grandmother's mind about fur? You should know by now that she digs in her heels when she thinks she's being attacked."

"I had to do *something*," I mumbled to the wall. "I couldn't just keep quiet. Selling fur coats should be against the law."

"But it's not. It's perfectly legal. So. You've gotten yourself into a big mess. Grandma Grace is steaming mad. The question is, what are you going to do about it now?"

Steaming mad. I ignored Mom's question. Hope surged through me as my heart thumped a steady beat: *We're going home, we're going home, we're going home!*

I turned back around to face Mom. I needed her on my side and I needed her to realize that going back to New Jersey would be the best thing for our family. Sitting up, I looked her straight in the eyes. "I'm sorry, Mom, I really am. But if Grandma Grace kicks us out of the house, we'll be okay. We can move back to New Jersey and you can go back to school there—"

"Whoa," Mom said, putting her hand out in front of her. A look passed across her face, as though she'd just figured out the answer to a complicated riddle. "Hold on a minute. No one said anything about getting kicked out—"

"But—but, I thought you said Grandma Grace is really angry. I bet she hates me for what I did. And there's nothing I can do to take it back—"

"Maybe not. But you can start by apologizing. Talk to your grandmother and explain why you feel so strongly about the issue. Tell her you didn't mean what you said about her, and that you do care about her." Mom put an arm around my shoulder. "You made a mistake, Sunny. But you can fix this."

I shrugged out from under my mom's arm. "No, Mom, she hates me!" I said, even though I didn't believe the words myself. My whole plan was falling apart, evaporating into the air, and I didn't know what I could do to put it back together. "She doesn't want me living here anymore. I'm sure of it!"

Mom gave me a little smile. And then she said the last words I wanted to hear: "The only thing I can tell you is you're not getting out of this one. It's up to you to fix things and make it right between the two of you again. And if you're hoping for an easy way out, you may as well give up on that idea. Grandma Grace would never go back on her word. She wouldn't do that to me, and she'd never do that to her grandchildren."

Tears seeped out of my eyes as I dropped back down on the bed, turning away from Mom as it all began to sink in.

Mom ran a hand over my hair. "You'll start with an apology," she said firmly. "And if you're afraid to face your grandmother, then you can put it in writing. I'm sure she's hurt by all of this, but one thing I'm learning about my mother is that underneath it all, she's really a softie."

I didn't say anything. I could imagine my grandmother taking an apology letter and tossing it in the trash can the way she'd done with the anti-fur pamphlet. Finally, Mom got up and left my room, closing the door behind her.

That's when the tears turned into ragged sobs, and I had to fight to catch my breath. What had I been thinking when I came up with my ridiculous plan? Had I completely lost my mind?

I'd been so mad at Mom for lying to me and messing up my whole life that I was ready to do whatever it took to get back home.

I'd forgotten, or ignored, the most important part: Grandma Grace wasn't really Cruella de Vil. She would never take away Mom's money for school and make us leave her house just because I made her angry.

Grandma Grace knew there were people who didn't like what she did for a living. She knew they would protest against her and would speak to reporters on TV if they got the chance.

But she didn't expect one of them to be her granddaughter. It would make people wonder about the person behind the shop and why she doesn't get along with her own family. It's the kind of thing people would gossip about, and I'm the one who caused it.

Not only had Sunny's Super-Stupendous Plan to Get Back Home totally self-destructed, but now I was stuck living with a grandmother who might never forgive me for what I'd done.

***

I was still up in my room, lying flat on my bed drowning in the hopelessness of my situation when I heard the front door open and shut. Grandma Grace was home.

I didn't want to get up from my bed. I thought maybe I could lie there for the rest of my life. But as voices floated up from the kitchen, I had a strong urge to hear what they were saying. I tiptoed into the hall and kneeled at the top of the steps.

At first, the conversation was polite chatter about where Grandma Grace had eaten and what movie she had seen. Then Mom said, "Sunny feels really badly about what happened."

I held my breath and had to let it back out before Grandma Grace spoke. "I've been thinking about this for the last few hours. All through dinner and the movie, too. Why didn't you tell me how Sunny felt about my selling furs?"

"I don't know. It wasn't too hard to pick up on. All those looks every time you mentioned your shop, how she acted when I actually made her go inside . . ."

"Okay, so maybe I was oblivious to it. But still, she could have come to me and told me how she felt."

"I'm afraid that's my fault. I discouraged her from saying anything. I thought it would cause a lot of tension between the two of you, when you were working hard to build a relationship—"

Grandma Grace sighed. "Oh, Rebecca. What kind of a person do you think I am? Did you really think I'd be angry at my own granddaughter for expressing her feelings? I may own a fur store, but I'm not an unreasonable person. I can see the big picture."

"Which is?"

"Family. Family is stronger than any disagreements we might have. I didn't realize that, Rebecca, until you and the girls came to stay with me."

Family. The word echoed in my heart.

Neither of them said anything for a minute.

"So, I'm trying to make sense of what's happened," Grandma Grace continued. "I can understand if Sunny feels strongly about the fur issue, but what I don't get is why she would attack me personally on TV. I mean, she's been harder to get to know, certainly, than Autumn, but I figured it was because she was older, more emotional. Was it all because of the fur store? Does she really hate me so much?"

My stomach clenched.

"Come on, Mom, you know she doesn't hate you."

"It sure felt like it, watching her up there on the TV screen."

"Well, I think you were on to something when you said she was harder to get to know than Autumn. Sunny's put up walls since we got here, and no, it's not just because she wishes you didn't own a fur store."

My heart skipped a beat.

"If you have a theory on all this," Grandma Grace said, "I'd love to hear it."

"Sunny was a hundred percent against moving in with you to begin with," Mom said. "I kept thinking she'd adjust, but ever since we got here, she has been thinking about how to get back home. I think Sunny was hoping she'd make you angry enough that you wouldn't let us stay."

I sucked in my breath.

"She thought I'd kick you out of the house?"

"Apparently."

"I thought she liked it here in Bennetsville. She seemed to be adjusting well, making new friends . . ."

"I think this has more to do with Scott than anything else," Mom said with a sigh. There was silence again. I balled up my fists, my fingernails digging into my palms.

"As you can see," Mom finally said, "Sunny and I have some issues we need to work out, too. But, in the meantime, she's gotten herself into quite a predicament and doesn't know what to do about it."

"And what would you like me to do?" Grandma Grace asked. "Tell her I forgive her and act like everything's perfectly normal?"

Yes, yes, yes! I squeezed my fists tighter. *Forgive me and move on!*

"No, of course not. Sunny needs to learn from her own mistakes. Like I told her, she needs to find a way to reach out to you."

"Exactly! I'm glad you told her that. You're a good mother, Rebecca. You know that, don't you?"

I turned and ran back to my room, not waiting to hear Mom's response.

CHAPTER TWENTY-SIX

The next morning I made a card for Grandma Grace. I painted a picture of daffodils, her favorite flower, on the front. On the inside I wrote:

Dear Grandma Grace,
I am sorry. I care about animals, but I shouldn't have gone to the protest.

Your granddaughter,
Sunny

I put the card in an envelope and left it in the mailbox with the other mail. Well, that was that. I'd done what Mom said I should do, and now it was up to my grandmother to decide if she ever wanted to forgive me.

Over the next couple of days, Grandma Grace spent a lot of time out of the house. When she was home, she spoke to me politely, but she never said anything to me about the card. I tried to avoid her as much as possible. It felt like the floor was littered with broken pieces of glass and both of us were trying not to step on any of them.

Mom and I didn't talk much either. She had said we had issues to work out, and I was waiting for her to bring them up. I guess I wasn't the only one trying to figure out what to do next.

I didn't feel like talking to Scott. Everything was too complicated to explain, and I knew Mom had already told him all about it, anyway. She'd taken the phone into the other room and closed the door when she called him, speaking so softly I couldn't make out a word. Not that I needed to.

That weekend, I served a lot of leftover turkey to Ripple. I also spent a lot of time in the backyard, swaying back and forth on the hammock as the cold November wind blew through me. *Now what? Now what?* The words echoed in my head with each creak of the hammock, and I didn't have any answers.

As I lay there staring up at the sky, I realized there was one more person I hadn't been honest with.

Lydia Applebaum. The person I'd been sitting with at lunch for the last two weeks, and practically my only friend at Evergreen.

I wondered if she would be angry that I hadn't told her the truth about my grandmother.

***

"Hey, I saw you on the news," said Holly, as I took my seat in front of her in language arts class on Monday morning.

I nodded, and sat down. Holly had never said a word to me before. I felt a tap on my shoulder, and turned back around. Holly gave me a big smile. "Was it exciting to be in a protest? Were you worried about getting arrested?"

"It's not against the law."

"Cool," she said, and then the girl who sat next to her started asking me questions until the bell rang and we had to be quiet.

Jessie, apparently, hadn't seen the protest. She chattered away in art class in her usual friendly way, but when it was time for lunch, she waved and walked off without me. After I sat with Lydia that first day, Jessie never asked me about it again. She probably wouldn't mind if I tried to sit with her, but she didn't seem to mind if I sat somewhere else either.

As I walked past Jessie's table a few minutes later, I noticed my seat had already been filled by a new friend, one of the other cheerleaders who had the straightest, blondest hair I'd ever seen.

I hesitated a minute before walking to Lydia's table. I'd been up all night thinking about what to say to her, and I had this bad feeling that the words would get all tangled up when I tried to explain. Finally, I took a deep breath.

"Hi, Lydia," I said in my friendliest voice.

She looked up at me. "Oh, hi," she said. Cool, like an arctic breeze. *Uh-oh.* "So I was just wondering, Sunny. Why have you been sitting with us lately? Did your other friends dump you?"

Heat prickled along my neck. The other girls at the table stopped talking and stared at me.

"Well, no . . . not exactly."

Lydia dipped her pita into hummus. "Because I was wondering if maybe they got mad because you didn't tell them the truth, either."

"I—I just wanted to sit with you. I thought we were friends—"

"*Were* is the correct form of the verb," Lydia said. "You know, the funny thing about grandmothers is sometimes you forget what they do for a living. For example, if your grandmother owned the fur store your friend was planning a protest against, you might just forget to mention it."

Sierra's eyes got really big. Jalia clamped a hand over her mouth. I looked down at my sneakers, rubbing my toe against the dirty cafeteria floor.

"About that," I said with a little fake laugh, "I didn't forget, exactly."

"You thought I'd never find out?"

"Not exactly that, either."

"So what was it then? When we saw the news, my mom couldn't believe it. She said she could get in big trouble if your parents didn't want you to participate because Mom's the one who contacted the media. You should have heard her! 'Why didn't you tell me Sunny's grandmother owned Luxury Furs and Leathers? I can't believe you encouraged her to protest against her own grandmother without talking to me about it first!' And when I told her you never told me, she thought *I* was the one who wasn't telling the truth!"

"I'm sorry, really I am! It's just, well, it's complicated."

Lydia put down her pita and looked right at me. "I'm listening."

"I thought it would be better if you didn't know—"

"It's not your fault your grandmother owns a fur store. But you should have trusted me."

"I know." The way she was looking at me, as if she really wanted to understand, made the words rush out of my mouth before I could stop them. "I thought about telling you, but I didn't even plan to go to the protest. I came to that first meeting because I was mad at my mom for lying to me, so I decided I could lie, too. And then, when I heard there were going to be reporters, I figured out the perfect solution to my problems. If I went on TV and said bad things about my grandmother, then she'd tell us we had to leave her house, and we could go back home to New Jersey." I stopped to take a breath. "So you can see why I couldn't talk to you about it. I didn't want to tell anyone. I was afraid I'd chicken out."

Lydia didn't say anything for a minute, but the look on her face had changed from understanding to something totally different. "You mean—you protested against your grandmother's store because you wanted to go home?"

I nodded. "It was a stupid plan. It didn't work."

"I can't believe this," Lydia said. "You weren't doing it for the animals? You were doing it for *yourself*?"

"No," I said, shaking my head. "I was doing it for the animals, too—"

"But I just heard you!" Pink circles had appeared on Lydia's cheeks and she looked angrier than I'd ever seen her. "You said you were doing it because you wanted to make your grandmother angry. You were using me and the protest to get what you wanted!"

"No," I said in my calmest voice, trying to get her to hear what I was saying. "Lydia, it's not like that. I wanted to help the animals—"

Lydia pushed back her chair and began packing up her lunch. "I don't have to listen to this. Are you coming?" she asked the other girls. They stood and followed behind her. I watched as they walked away, leaving me alone at the empty table, the same way I'd left Lydia when she'd brought ratatouille for lunch a couple of months ago.

I sank down into an empty chair, dropping my head on my arms. There were mess-ups and there were *mess-ups*. This was the kind that just kept getting worse and worse. It was like the time I was mowing the grass and a rock hit the window. At first it was a little hole. Then I heard a crackling noise and lines starting shooting down from the hole and, before I knew it, the glass shattered and the window fell into a million pieces.

Except this time, it felt like I was the one cracking.

CHAPTER TWENTY-SEVEN

Sunny, is that you?" Mom called from the sunroom when I got home that afternoon.

"Yeah, it's me."

"There's someone here to see you."

I dropped my book bag on the floor with a loud thud. I didn't feel like talking, and I didn't want to face my usual Evergreen load of homework either. All I really wanted to do was climb back in bed and pull the covers up over my head.

I dragged my feet as I walked to the sunroom, hoping I could get away quickly.

Then I heard his voice.

"Scott?" I took off at a run, straight for his arms. As I collapsed into him, all the bad feelings from my horrible day melted away. I didn't ever want to let go.

Finally, I took a step back. He still looked exactly the same, just like he was supposed to. "What are you doing here? I thought you weren't coming until Christmas."

"Changed my mind," Scott said with a grin.

"Thanks," I said. Mom must have declared an emergency if Scott was here. But I was glad just the same.

"So how was your day?" he asked, like it was perfectly normal that he was sitting on the wicker couch in Grandma Grace's sunroom.

I sat down in the rocking chair across from him. "It stunk."

"What happened?" Scott asked.

"Everyone hates me."

"Everyone at school?" Mom asked. "What are you talking about?"

"Well, Jessie's not really my friend anymore, and Lydia won't talk to me because she says I was using her and the animals for my own selfish purposes."

"Why does Lydia think you were using her?" Scott asked.

"I don't feel like talking about it," I said.

"Whatever you say," Scott replied. "We've got plenty of time for talking."

"Really? How long are you staying?"

"I flew in this morning, and I'm flying back on Thursday."

"You can't even stay the weekend?"

He shook his head. "Not this time. I've got the shop covered for the next few days, but it was last-minute planning. I need to get back."

I rocked back on the chair. Hard.

"Wish I could stay longer. But I'll be back for Christmas."

I rocked some more.

"Your mom and I were thinking it wouldn't hurt for you to miss a day of school. She said there's a great place to go horseback riding around here if it's not too cold."

"Ridge Gap Trail?"

Mom nodded.

"Really? You'll let me miss school?"

"It would be good for the two of you to have some time to talk," Mom said.

I looked at Scott. "Just us? What about Autumn?"

Scott said. "Your mom and I will talk to Autumn later."

I thought about that. Autumn wasn't going to be happy when she found out we went horseback riding without her, but I liked the idea of having Scott to myself.

The door squeaked open and I heard the thump of a book bag being dropped in the front hall. "Mom?" Autumn's voice rang out as she closed the door behind her. "I'm home!"

"Let's plan on Wednesday," Scott said with a wink as my sister ran into the room and threw herself into his arms.

***

My TV fame only lasted one day; I went to class on Tuesday and no one asked any more questions. On Wednesday morning, I woke up to the sun shining through my curtains and spilling onto the floor. I pulled up my blinds and looked out at a blue-sky December day. I jumped out of bed and pulled on my clothes, glad that I didn't have to face another day sitting alone at lunch.

A little while later, Scott and I drove to Ridge Gap Trail. We talked about teachers and schoolwork, avoiding tough subjects like losing friends, parents who keep the truth from you, and what happens after you protest against your grandmother's store.

After a three-mile hike through the woods and a horseback ride on Ridge Gap Trail, we ended up at Sollecito's for lunch. I pulled off my gloves and rubbed my hands together before reaching for a piece of warm bread from the basket.

Scott passed me a plate of olive oil and spices. "I'll say one thing for Grandma Grace. She sure knows how to pick a beautiful place to live."

I gazed out the windows of the café, taking in the blue haze of the mountains; I knew exactly what he meant.

"So," Scott said after the waitress came and took our order, "I guess it's time for us to talk."

I sat up straighter. I knew he wasn't angry with me the way Mom had been. He mostly seemed worried. He must have felt pretty rotten about keeping the truth from me, or he wouldn't have flown all the way down here in the middle of the week.

"I know you were angry after you found the photo," Scott said. "Especially when you wouldn't talk to me for the first few days. I don't blame you—I would have been plenty mad, too."

I shrugged. "It was mostly Mom's fault. She's the one who lied about the photo when I asked her about it earlier."

"It was *both* our faults. We should have explained the situation sooner. So when your mom called me about the protest, I knew I needed to come right away. It just isn't like you, Sunny. You've always had such a big heart and you've never hurt anyone purposely before."

I looked down at my plate, my stomach twisting like a wet towel you want to wring out. Scott always called me softhearted and said that I couldn't hurt a fly, which is why he escorted creepy crawlies out of the house for me instead of killing them.

"I didn't mean to hurt Grandma Grace." But the words didn't make sense, not even to me. "I wasn't really thinking about her feelings. I was just thinking about getting back home."

"I know. Your mom figured that out pretty quick. We'd really messed up good, keeping secrets from you like that."

Pushing the bread around in the olive oil, I felt a tiny drop of hope bubble up inside of me.

The bubble burst with Scott's next words.

"Even though it was wrong of us to keep the truth from you, that didn't make it okay for you to lie to your mom or to sneak around without asking permission or, even worse, treat your grandmother disrespectfully. That's not who you are, Sunflower. Your mother and I are both disappointed in you."

The words settled in the bottom of my stomach like a hollow peach pit. Now I knew exactly what Mom had tried to tell me: acting out would not get me what I wanted. It only meant I had to live with the consequences.

I was glad when the waitress arrived with our food. It was easier to pay attention to my lunch than to say what I needed to. I took a bite of ravioli and burned my tongue.

"I'm sorry," I whispered as I swallowed back tears. "I really am."

Scott squeezed my shoulder. "I know, honey. And I'm sorry, too."

We ate in silence for a few minutes, though between my burnt tongue and my guilty conscience I barely tasted my food.

"Anyway, I've been thinking about all this," Scott said, putting his fork down. "I know we've all made a lot of mistakes. Your mom and I should have made sure you knew we weren't really a couple. What I need you to understand is that we didn't think it mattered."

"You and Mom keep saying that, but I don't get it. How could you think it didn't matter?"

Scott shook his head. "We really were a happy family. We weren't secretly arguing when you girls weren't around. Your mom and I have always been best friends. We didn't think it mattered if we loved each other as friends or loved each other as something more. I mean, love is love, right?"

I shrugged. Maybe this wasn't about wanting a job change and Mom pursuing her dreams. If it was, she could have gotten her MFA at home in New Jersey. "Maybe Mom decided that best friends love wasn't enough," I finally said.

Scott gazed out the window, at the blue mountain tops covered with clouds. "And maybe she wasn't just thinking of herself," he said quietly.

"Well, she wasn't thinking of us!" I said, then clapped my hand over my mouth. Mom thought it was time for Scott to look for a new girlfriend?

Scott looked back at me and nodded. "We'd always thought it was enough. But maybe your mom's right. We both owe it to ourselves to find out if there's more."

"But—but what's going to happen to me? To me and Autumn?" The words tumbled out, words I'd been holding back for so long. "Mom says we might move back to New Jersey when she finishes her program and we might not. She said we'll have to wait and see! But it's not like you adopted me or that you and Mom were married and you're getting a divorce. Then, at least you'd have to see me a couple of times a year, no matter where we moved." I slumped back against my chair. I felt a little like that milk carton I'd once dropped on the floor and punctured, the milk spurting out everywhere like a fountain.

Scott's eyes widened.

"What?" I asked.

"It's just"—he shook his head—"I guess I'm a little dense about things. Sunflower, I need you to listen to me." He reached across the table and squeezed my hand. "It doesn't matter whether your mom and I are together. It doesn't matter if my name is on your adoption certificate or whether your mom and I were once married and now we're divorced. I don't need a custody letter to tell me when I can visit my own daughter. I love you and your sister more than anyone else in the world, and that is never going to change. Okay?"

I nodded, tears filling my eyes. "Okay." I may have wanted things to turn out differently, but for now, holding Scott's hand and believing that he would always be there for me would have to be enough.

**

Mom and Scott took Autumn out for dinner by herself that evening. She knew I'd stayed home to spend some time with

Scott that day, but she figured it was because of all the trouble I'd gotten into and she didn't protest too much about it.

I decided it was best not to mention Ridge Gap Trail.

They were gone for almost two hours. I heard the front door open around 7:45, followed by the pound of Autumn's feet on the stairs. I looked up from my sketchbook when I heard her stop at my doorway.

"How was dinner?" I asked.

"Great! We went to Burger-Rama and Scott let me order a large order of cheese fries *and* onion rings! Then we stopped at Menchies for frozen yogurt. I got chocolate and cheesecake and a ton of toppings."

"Lucky," I said.

"Too bad you had to stay home with Grandma Grace. I bet you had to eat something super healthy."

I shrugged. "It was okay. We had Lean Cuisines, and she let us eat in front of the TV."

Autumn's mouth dropped open. "In the living room?"

"Yup. Grandma Grace has these special folding tables. I guess she used to eat in front of the TV all the time, before we came along."

"Well, I'm asking her if she'll let me use one next time," Autumn said.

"Don't press your luck." I knew the real reason we used the folding tables was so we didn't have to fill up the silence between us. "Besides, you got to have a junk food dinner. There were probably TVs all over the restaurant."

"That's true." She stood there in the doorway a minute like she wanted to say something, not coming in but not leaving either. "What are you working on?"

I held up my sketchbook, showing her the picture of a cat with caramel swirls.

Autumn's eyes widened. "Is that the little cat you've been feeding in Grandma's backyard?"

I shook my head, and looked back down at the picture. "It's just a random drawing—"

"Ha! I know you've been feeding that kitty. You can't fool me. You're just like Mom and Scott. They think I'm too young to pay attention, that I don't have any idea what's going on, but they're wrong. Everyone acts like I'm stupid or something."

"I didn't say you were stupid."

"No, but you didn't tell me about the cat."

"What did Mom and Scott tell you? At dinner, I mean."

Autumn crossed her arms in front of her chest. "Mom said they were splitting up."

I put my sketchbook down on my desk. "Mom said that?"

"Well, she said they were still friends, that they'd always be friends, and that we'd always be a family. But she said they're not going to be a couple anymore." Autumn bit her lip, and tears swam in her eyes.

I jumped up from my seat and put my arm around her. "It's going to be okay."

She shrugged my arm away and swiped at her eyes. "I know that, Sunny. I told you, I know things. Of course they're splitting up. Why else would Mom move us all the way down here?"

"Bennetsville's not such a bad place to live," I found myself saying. "And Scott's always going to be our dad, no matter where he lives."

Autumn nodded, and sniffed. "I know," she said. "I just wish—I just wish things were different."

This time I was the one nodding. "I know," I said. "Me, too."

CHAPTER TWENTY-EIGHT

From: MadelineL@ilovebooks.com
To: SunnyKid@CreativityisCool.com
WHERE ARE YOU????

SUNNY! What's going on? Is everything okay? I haven't heard from you in a looong time. Did you get my Thanksgiving card? Miss you so much!

XOXO,
Maddy

P.S. Are you mad at me? Please, please write back.

Scott left the next morning. We had a long talk about Grandma Grace, and I knew it was up to me to make things right. *This weekend*, I told myself. I couldn't put it off any longer. Giving her a brief apology card because Mom made me didn't take the place of a real apology that I meant.

Somehow, I got through the rest of the week. Lydia ignored me, Jessie's table was overflowing with new cheerleaders, and I started getting used to sitting in the back of the cafeteria with my sketchbook again.

On Saturday afternoon, Mom dropped me off at Lydia's for the OM meeting. After knocking a few times, I opened the door and walked inside.

"Hi, Sunny," Mrs. Applebaum called from the kitchen. "Everyone's already downstairs—you know the way."

"Okay," I said as I slipped past her. She hadn't mentioned the protest, so I wasn't going to bring it up, either.

Coach Baker had already started a hands-on warm-up that involved tape, toothpicks, and rubber bands. I sat down next to Jalia and tried to help, but the first rubber band shot across the room and the next one broke in half.

I walked over to pick up the rubber band when one of the posters tacked to the wall caught my eye. It was a picture of a unicorn leaping through the clouds, and it said: NOTHING IS IMPOSSIBLE. THE WORD ITSELF SAYS I'M POSSIBLE.

I sat back down with the rubber band and thought about the poster while my teammates worked. It was one of those things grown-ups might say to kids, and I wondered how to make it true. I couldn't change how Mom felt about Scott, I couldn't get Grandma Grace to change her mind about furs, and I couldn't get Mom to move us back to New Jersey no matter how hard I tried.

But over the last week, I'd been thinking a lot. I'd been wanting the change to come from other people, but maybe the change needed to come from me. I could trust Scott when he told me how much he loved me and that he'd never forget about me, no matter how far apart we might live from each other. I could get to know my grandmother better even if she owned a fur store, something I was against. I could forgive my mom for not being honest with me and believe her when she said she did it because she wanted to give us a family with two parents.

And I could make friends in Bennetsville, or at least learn to be a better friend to someone who had trusted me.

It had been a week since Fur-Free Friday. A whole week of no friends, of tiptoeing around family members . . . and of feeling sorry for myself.

Maybe I was still like Annalise, taking the easy way out instead of facing my own problems. I looked over at Lydia while we did the group cheer.

It was time for things to change.

CHAPTER TWENTY-NINE

When I got home from the meeting Saturday afternoon, the first thing I noticed was the vase in the middle of the table. My beautifully decoupaged vase filled with fresh flowers!

"Did your secret admirer send you more flowers?" I asked, laughing.

Mom dropped her keys on the counter. "Actually, the flowers are from one of my critique partners."

I hesitated. "Jeb?"

"Another critique partner who's been meeting with us," Mom said. "Her name's Caroline."

"Oh." Her answer immediately made me feel better. But just because it was Caroline this time didn't mean that Jeb wasn't waiting with flowers around the corner.

Mom patted the seat next to her. "I've been thinking about that secret admirer. Strange how he only sent one gift, and then I never heard from him again."

"Maybe he gave up."

"It really is a gorgeous vase. Someone went to a lot of trouble to decorate the bottle, someone who's very artistic. And you know what else I noticed? Those roses looked just like the ones in Mrs. Wright's backyard. Isn't that funny?" She winked at me.

"Not really." I sank into a chair. "When did you figure it out?"

Mom smiled. "You could say I had a hunch right away."

"But you didn't say anything—"

"I thought I'd wait to see what happened. Why'd you do it? I know it wasn't just to brighten my day, which it definitely did."

I sighed. "It was part of Sunny's Super-Stupendous Plan to Get Mom and Dad Back Together. Which totally failed."

Mom's eyebrows crinkled. "Sunny's Super . . . what?"

"Stupendous Plan. I thought the only thing missing between you and Scott was romance. So I came up with a bunch of ideas to get you to fall madly in love again—"

"That's what it was all about? The photos of Scott all over the house? The playlists? The photo album?"

"And the makeover."

Mom laughed. "I had no idea . . . Guess that shows how much I'm living in my own little world."

"I sent the makeover photo to Scott, but he didn't really say anything about it. Then he sent that photo of Mark to me by accident, when I asked for pictures for the album . . . and once I figured out there was nothing I could do to get you and Scott back together, I changed my plan. That's when I came up with Sunny's Super-Stupendous Plan to Get Back Home. Only it wasn't so stupendous."

"Oh, honey . . ." Mom put an arm around my shoulder and gave me a little hug. "I'm so sorry. I should have been honest with you from the start."

We didn't say anything for a minute, just sat there staring at my vase filled with colorful flowers. Finally, I reached forward and touched a sunflower. "It's pretty," I said.

"Yes," Mom said. "Sunflowers are pretty . . . and strong. You know why I named you Sunflower?"

I shrugged, even though Mom had told me before.

"It's because they show resilience. They always follow the sun and always stand proud and tall. Just like you, Sunny. I know things have been hard for you lately, and I've—*we've* —made a lot of mistakes. But you'll get through all this and you'll be just fine."

I nodded, wanting with all my heart to believe her.

"So, how was practice this afternoon?" Mom asked.

I looked away from the sunflowers, glad that she'd changed the subject. "Good. Um . . . I was wondering, do you think we could stop by Earthly Goods sometime?"

"Did you and Lydia make up?"

I shook my head. "Not yet."

A grin spread across my mom's face and she picked up her keys. "Well, no time like the present. I've always wanted to buy some of that tofu ice cream they have! What are we waiting for?"

CHAPTER THIRTY

Lydia's eyebrows went up when we walked into Earthly Goods. I waved at her and she waved back. I took that as a good sign.

After we picked out our Tofutti from the cooler, Mom said she wanted to look at the natural soaps and lotions, so I headed back to the front of the store. "Hi," I said as I walked up to the counter.

"Hi," Lydia said.

"I had a craving for Tofutti."

"You came to the right place then. Did you see the new flavors?"

I waited until she finished listing flavors, and then I knew I couldn't wait any longer. "Look, Lydia, I'm sorry. I'm sorry I didn't tell you the truth about my grandmother, and I'm sorry if you think I was using you by joining the protest. I hate that my grandmother sells fur coats, but I didn't know what to do about it. Still, even though I was upset about the coats, I was more upset about my parents. My mom and dad—well, his name's Scott and they're not married—actually, I'm adopted, but only by Mom. But anyway, I wanted them to get back together. I tried all kinds of things and nothing worked and I found out there was nothing keeping them together, and that's when I knew I had to get back home, so Scott couldn't forget me." I stopped to catch my breath.

Lydia didn't say anything for a while. Finally she nodded. "The protest was your ticket home."

"Yeah." I dropped my head.

Lydia put her hand on my shoulder. "I'm sorry about your parents."

I looked back up at her. "Me, too. And I'm sorry about the ratatouille. I should never have followed Jessie and those girls just because you brought some stinky food, and I should have given you a chance earlier—"

"It's okay, Sunny. I forgive you."

Mom picked that exact moment to walk up with the groceries. She chatted to Lydia about recipes like she hadn't even noticed we were having an important conversation.

"Nice seeing you, Mrs. Beringer," Lydia said after Mom had paid. She looked over at me. "Hope you enjoy your Tofutti!"

"Thanks," I said, then paused. "See you Monday?"

"Sure," Lydia said. "You can sit with us if you want, but I'm warning you—I'm bringing ratatouille."

"That's all right," I said quickly.

A big grin stretched across Lydia's face. "Just kidding! I'm not that crazy about eggplant, either."

I burst out laughing and Lydia joined me. Mom looked at both of us like we'd lost our minds. "What's so funny about eggplant?"

I was laughing too hard to answer.

"It looks a little gross!" Lydia finally said, which sent us off into another fit of giggles.

"I take it you've made up?" Mom asked on the way home. "You're friends again?"

"Yeah." I settled back in my seat. A lot of things hadn't worked out the way I'd planned. But even though I never expected to be friends with Lydia, it turned out to be exactly what I needed.

CHAPTER THIRTY-ONE

From: SunnyKid@CreativityisCool.com
To: MadelineL@ilovebooks.com
Sorry I Haven't Written!

Hi Maddy! I'm really sorry I haven't written in a while. Yes, I got the picture of you and Emma dressed up as witches, and yes, I guess I was a little mad at you. I moved away and you got a new best friend—*snap*—just like that. And it made me really sad, especially since it's hard making new friends over here.

Things got a little crazy for a while, but now it's getting better. I've actually made a new friend, too. I will tell you the whole story someday if you have time. Hint: It has something to do with my grandma's fur store. All I can say is moving to a new place has *not* been easy!

I'm working on a Happy Holidays card for you and I'll send it soon.

Sunflower

From: MadelineL@ilovebooks.com
To: SunnyKid@CreativityisCool.com
Re: Sorry I Haven't Written!

Sunflower!!!!! I like that you signed your old name. You are still my best friend, and always will be. Mom says we can set up a time to FaceTime. Then you can tell me the whole story. I can't wait to talk to you!!!

XOXOXO,
Madeline

When I got home from school on Monday afternoon, I knew it was time to talk to my grandmother. I'd been learning to be tough and resilient, like my name, by asking my parents serious questions and learning to accept the answers. It also meant doing things I was uncomfortable with, like apologizing to Lydia and trying to explain things to my grandmother.

Silently rehearsing what I'd say to Grandma Grace, I took the plate of tuna fish to the far corner of the yard to feed Ripple like I had every afternoon when I came home. But she didn't come running and I didn't hear a rustle of leaves and branches.

I stopped thinking about Grandma's furs and cupped my hands over my mouth. "Ripple! Come here, kitty kitty!"

No response. I called again, louder this time. But I didn't see her, and all I could hear was the wind blowing through the trees. My stomach churned. Something was wrong. Ripple always came when I called for her. I bent down on my knees and peered under the bushes.

If I didn't know the cat's brown and gold markings well, I would never have spotted her in the underbrush.

"Ripple?" My voice came out in a whisper. She didn't move. I crept closer to her, my hand shaking as I parted the leaves. One of her eyes was swollen shut and dried blood matted her fur. She let out a weak mew, so soft I could barely hear it.

I got up and raced toward the house, my heart pounding louder than my tennis shoes hitting the grass.

"Mom! Mom!" I yelled as I burst in the back door, letting it slam behind me.

Grandma Grace rushed into the kitchen. "Sunny? What is it?"

I glanced out the window and noticed the jeep was gone. "Where's Mom?"

"She left to run a few errands. What's wrong? Maybe I can help."

I shifted my weight from one foot to the other, leaning against a kitchen chair. "It's—it's my cat."

My grandmother's eyebrows shot up. "Your cat?"

I nodded. "I mean, she's not actually my cat—Mom made us leave Stellaluna at home. But it's a stray I've been taking care of, and she's really hurt. We need to get her to the vet right now. I promise I'll pay you back—"

"Let's not worry about that now." Grandma Grace headed out to the utility porch, where she found a box and an old blanket. "Okay, now where's this cat of yours?"

I was out the door and across the yard in three leaps. I bent down on the grass, finding Ripple in the exact spot I'd left her. "Ripple," I said softly, "I'm going to help you. Then you'll feel good as new."

My grandmother's heels dug into the dirt as she came closer and kneeled down next to me. The cat blinked at me with her one good eye. She didn't struggle as I slipped my arms beneath her and placed her in the box.

"I heard barking last night," Grandma Grace said. "I woke up and looked out my window. There were a couple of big black dogs running across the yard. I went downstairs and banged on the back door to get them to leave."

I looked down at Ripple lying so still in the box, her fur caked with blood. Her eyes were closed and her tail didn't even flicker. I swallowed. "I bet they attacked her."

"A couple of aggressive dogs can kill a cat when they gang up," Grandma Grace said. "Let me just give your mom a call so she'll be back when Autumn gets home, and then we'll be on our way."

I bit my lip as my grandmother picked up the phone. *Hurry, hurry, hurry!*

"How long have you known this cat?" Grandma Grace asked when we pulled out of the driveway a few minutes later.

"Since we moved here." I stroked Ripple's head. "She's been hanging around the yard."

"I guess your old grandmother's a little dense when it comes to hints," she said as we stopped at a light.

I shrugged. If Mom had been driving, she would have gone straight through the yellow. We took off again, slow and steady. I looked over at the speedometer. "Can't you drive a little faster?"

"I'm going the speed limit, Sunny, even if your mom doesn't believe in it."

I slumped back in my seat with a sigh.

"Anyway, as I was saying, I should have paid more attention, and not just about the cat. You hated that I sold fur coats from the moment you found out."

"Um, yeah." I gripped the box tightly, watching my knuckles turn white. I'd been planning how I was going to bring up the subject for a week, and now my grandmother was making it easier on me. But I couldn't concentrate on anything except the cat on my lap, the cat who might die if we didn't get her to the vet soon.

Grandma Grace had both hands up on the steering wheel, her eyes fixed on the road ahead. "Still, I was totally unprepared. Seeing you up on the screen was a shock, and when you lashed out at me—"

"I'm sorry! I didn't know what else to do. I didn't want to hurt your feelings, honest! I wanted to speak up for the animals, so at first I was just going to wear the costume to the protest and no one would have ever found out. But then I realized that getting back to New Jersey was more important than anything else in the world, so that's when I decided to speak to the lady on TV. I was just trying to make you mad enough to send us home. That's all I wanted. To go home. I'm sorry if you hate me—" My voice broke and I looked down at Ripple, her brown and caramel swirls blurring in front of me.

"Oh, Sunny." My grandmother shook her head. "I could never hate you. You're my granddaughter." She took her hand off the steering wheel and patted my hand. Then her foot went down on the accelerator and when I looked up at the speedometer, we were going five miles over the speed limit.

CHAPTER THIRTY-TWO

Let me be honest with you," the doctor said an hour later, after he'd taken Ripple to an examining room. "This cat's been hurt badly. She's lost a lot of blood and probably has some internal injuries. She'll need surgery, and even with that, there's no guarantee she'll make it."

I gripped the counter in front of me. *Ripple will make it. She just has to.*

"You'll have to make up your mind if you want to take a chance with the surgery," the doctor continued. "It can be quite expensive when we see an animal with these kind of injuries. I can work up a quote, and then you can decide what you want to do."

I was afraid to look at my grandmother. I concentrated on taking slow, easy breaths. My eyes rested on a photo of

Dr. Wenton and a large, happy dog. He seemed like a nice enough person, one who loved animals. Maybe he'd let me work off the bill by helping around the clinic.

I could picture myself, wearing a white lab coat, feeding the animals that stayed overnight, walking dogs, cheering up lonely cats.

"There's no time to wait for a quote," Grandma Grace said, taking out her credit card and handing it to the doctor. "This animal needs help right away."

I turned to face my grandmother, the last person I would have expected to try to save a cat's life. "Thank you," I said, my voice coming out in a whisper.

"Don't worry, you'll pay me back. I've got plenty of chores that need doing around the house," she said with a wink.

I nodded, thinking about how I'd been planning on asking her about chores to earn money for Mom and Scott's gift certificate but hadn't because I hadn't thought she'd pay me a penny. Who would have guessed she'd let me do chores to pay off a vet bill for a cat she hadn't even known about? "I'll get started right away."

***

Autumn was waiting for us on the front porch when we pulled into the driveway. "Is it the stray who's been hanging around the yard?" she asked me. "I knew you were feeding her, even if you said you weren't. I saw the saucers under the bushes. Why didn't you tell me the truth?"

I glanced over at my grandmother. "It was a secret."

"What happened to her? Is she going to be okay?"

"She was attacked by a dog. Or probably a bunch of dogs."

"The doctor's doing everything he can," Grandma Grace said, putting a hand on my shoulder.

I swallowed, trying not to think about what was happening back at the doctor's office. What I needed was to stay busy. "I'm going to work on some chores to help pay for the vet bill. You can help if you want," I told Autumn.

And she did. Silver tea sets and candlesticks needed polishing, drawers needed organizing, a porch needed sweeping, windows needed scrubbing, and rooms needed dusting and vacuuming. I worked on the list all the next day, sometimes with my sister's help and sometimes without. I didn't stop thinking about Ripple the whole time.

The phone rang late Saturday afternoon.

"Oh, hello, Dr. Wenton," I heard my grandmother say. I dropped my dust rag on the floor and ran into the kitchen, my legs shaking as I stood next to her.

"Uh-huh. Hmm. Uh-huh!"

"What is it?" I asked. "Is Ripple going to be okay?"

"Just a minute. My granddaughter is hopping around on one foot waiting to find out how her cat is." Grandma Grace held her hand over the receiver. "She made it through the surgery with flying colors—"

"Yippee!" I jumped up and down, pumping my arms in the air, and Autumn joined in. *"Yahoo!"*

"Just a minute. Girls, I can't hear the doctor."

We both quieted down. I rocked back and forth on my toes, listening to some more uh-huhs and ahas before my grandmother finally said, "Thank you, Doctor. We appreciate all your hard work."

Mom walked into the kitchen as my grandmother hung up the phone. "Good news?"

"The best," I said. "Ripple's going to be okay!"

"The doctor says she needs more rest," Grandma Grace said, "but he thinks she's on her way to a full recovery."

"How many more nights does she have to stay at the vet?" I asked.

"He wants to keep an eye on her for the next few days."

"I hate to bring this up," Mom said. "But have you thought about what's going to happen to the cat after that? I'm sure the doctor will want her to spend some time inside . . ."

"Can she stay on the porch?" I asked. "We could fix up a bed for her there."

"It gets pretty cold out there at night," Grandma Grace said. "She'll need to stay in the house, at least while she's recovering."

"Does that mean we can keep her?" Autumn asked.

I held my breath.

"Of course," Grandma Grace said. "Believe it or not, I happen to like cats."

I felt my eyes opening wide. "Really?"

"Don't be so surprised," Grandma Grace said with a wink. "Besides, we're already paying the vet bills so this cat is officially yours to keep."

"Thanks so much, Grandma Grace. I can't wait to bring her home." I threw my arms around her and felt her arms encircling me, hugging me back.

From: SunnyKid@CreativityisCool.com
To: Scott@BookBuyers.com
Grandma Grace, the cat lover!

Dear Scott,

Guess what? I have a new cat. Her name is Ripple (after your favorite song) and she has fur the color of fudge stripe ice cream. She got attacked by dogs, but Grandma Grace paid for the vet bill. (Don't worry. I'm working it off.) She's coming home tomorrow. Yes, that's right. Grandma Grace said she likes cats! Maybe there is hope for her after all.

So, anyway, I have the greatest news. I talked to Grandma Grace about Stellaluna and she said we should never have left her at home. We're all hoping you can fly her down here when you come to visit next week. Lydia flew her three cats all the way from California and one of them is fourteen, the same as Stellaluna, so I'm sure she'll be fine. I just know Stellaluna and Ripple are going to be the best of friends. I can't wait to see her . . . and you!

Love,
Sunflower

P.S. Mark your calendar for Saturday, March 3, the regional Odyssey of the Mind competition. You can't miss it!!!

ACKNOWLEDGMENTS

I have many people to thank, who have helped me along the way as I transformed my manuscript from idea to book-on-the-shelf:

My amazing agent Brent Taylor, who has been steadfast in his enthusiasm and support since I first sent him *Call Me Sunflower* and he read it overnight. His encouragement and positive energy have inspired me to become a better writer.

My incredible editor Alison Weiss who reminds me of Ms. Rusgo, teaching me to "dig deep" with my characters and "Emote, emote, emote!" *Call Me Sunflower* wouldn't be what it is today without her thoughtful feedback and expert guidance.

My fantastic writer friends, for providing honest feedback, encouragement, and virtual chocolates and wine on those tough days when I've needed them: Karen Bly, Melody

Delgado, Eileen Feldsott, Stephanie Gorin, Katie Kennedy, Kim Small Lyng, Joseph Miller, Marilou Reeder, and Yolanda Ridge.

My best friend Liz and her girls Nicole, Danielle, and Alexandra, for sending me hearts and sunflowers and being my cheerleaders!

Naomi Moore, for being my first reader, for all her positive feedback, for being there on those tough days just to listen. I'm lucky to have Naomi as my sister!

My mom, for showing me just how strong and resilient she is now that she's standing tall on her own after having my dad by her side for more than 50 years.

Eliana and Carissa, for inspiring me with their never-ending supply of creativity. Eliana, thank you for allowing me the privilege of being your Odyssey of the Mind coach for the past four years! Up to the rooftops!

Scott, for his unconditional love and support throughout this long writing journey.

To all my other friends and family who celebrated the release of my debut novel, *Extraordinary*; for buying the book and telling me it touched your heart, for writing reviews, giving it as gifts, and letting other people know how much you liked it. This means the world to me.

And to Margaret Franklin, who couldn't have been happier for me when *Extraordinary* hit the shelves and cheered for me every step of the way. You are greatly missed.